Crossing the Line

Somebody's knuckles rapped at the door. Slocum made a face and thought, *If that's Will, I'm gonna kill him.*

But he pulled on his britches, tossed a sheet over Mandy, and went to the door. He opened it to find a familiar face, but it wasn't Will's.

"Wyatt!" Slocum exclaimed. "You old dog! Glad to see you. I'd invite you in, but—"

Wyatt didn't wait for him to finish the sentence. He just barged into the room and said, "Slocum, old buddy, I'm glad to see you, too, but I need your help. Bronc Dugan broke out last night. He somehow thumped Morgan and let himself out, then walked down to the livery, stole a horse, and left. Went south, we think."

"Got to wake up my partner and grab some breakfast," Slocum said, fingering his chin. "Half an hour all right?"

"Yeah," said Wyatt. He turned and put his hand on the knob, before he looked back. "Oh, by the way, Slocum, that horse Dugan stole?"

"Yeah?"

"He was yours."

DON'T MISS THESE
ALL-ACTION WESTERN SERIES
FROM THE BERKLEY PUBLISHING GROUP

THE GUNSMITH by J. R. Roberts
Clint Adams was a legend among lawmen, outlaws, and
ladies. They called him . . . the Gunsmith.

LONGARM by Tabor Evans
The popular long-running series about Deputy U.S. Marshal
Custis Long—his life, his loves, his fight for justice.

SLOCUM by Jake Logan
Today's longest-running action Western. John Slocum rides a
deadly trail of hot blood and cold steel.

BUSHWHACKERS by B. J. Lanagan
An action-packed series by the creators of Longarm! The
rousing adventures of the most brutal gang of cutthroats ever
assembled—Quantrill's Raiders.

DIAMONDBACK by Guy Brewer
Dex Yancey is Diamondback, a Southern gentleman turned
con man when his brother cheats him out of the family for-
tune. Ladies love him. Gamblers hate him. But nobody pulls
one over on Dex . . .

WILDGUN by Jack Hanson
The blazing adventures of mountain man Will Barlow—
from the creators of Longarm!

TEXAS TRACKER by Tom Calhoun
J.T. Law: the most relentless—and dangerous—manhunter
in all Texas. Where sheriffs and posses fail, he's the best man
to bring in the most vicious outlaws—for a price.

JAKE LOGAN

SLOCUM AND THE SONORAN FUGITIVE

JOVE BOOKS, NEW YORK

THE BERKLEY PUBLISHING GROUP
Published by the Penguin Group
Penguin Group (USA) Inc.
375 Hudson Street, New York, New York 10014, USA
Penguin Group (Canada), 90 Eglinton Avenue East, Suite 700, Toronto, Ontario M4P 2Y3, Canada
(a division of Pearson Penguin Canada Inc.)
Penguin Books Ltd., 80 Strand, London WC2R 0RL, England
Penguin Group Ireland, 25 St. Stephen's Green, Dublin 2, Ireland (a division of Penguin Books Ltd.)
Penguin Group (Australia), 250 Camberwell Road, Camberwell, Victoria 3124, Australia
(a division of Pearson Australia Group Pty. Ltd.)
Penguin Books India Pvt. Ltd., 11 Community Centre, Panchsheel Park, New Delhi—110 017, India
Penguin Group (NZ), 67 Apollo Drive, Rosedale, North Shore 0632, New Zealand
(a division of Pearson New Zealand Ltd.)
Penguin Books (South Africa) (Pty.) Ltd., 24 Sturdee Avenue, Rosebank, Johannesburg 2196,
South Africa

Penguin Books Ltd., Registered Offices: 80 Strand, London WC2R 0RL, England

This is a work of fiction. Names, characters, places, and incidents either are the product of the author's imagination or are used fictitiously, and any resemblance to actual persons, living or dead, business establishments, events, or locales is entirely coincidental.

SLOCUM AND THE SONORAN FUGITIVE

A Jove Book / published by arrangement with the author

PRINTING HISTORY
Jove edition / February 2010

Copyright © 2010 by Penguin Group (USA) Inc.
Cover illustration by Sergio Giovine.

ISBN: 978-0-515-14756-8

JOVE®
Jove Books are published by The Berkley Publishing Group,
a division of Penguin Group (USA) Inc.
375 Hudson Street, New York, New York 10014.
JOVE® is a registered trademark of Penguin Group (USA) Inc.
The "J" design is a trademark of Penguin Group (USA) Inc.

PRINTED IN THE UNITED STATES OF AMERICA

10 9 8 7 6 5 4 3 2 1

1

Slocum was off Apache and running for cover the second he heard the slug sing out. He dropped behind the first big boulder he came to, and slid to a stop just as the second slug sang off the rocks behind him.

He brought up his rifle and placed a shot right where he'd seen the first one come from, before he twisted his head, checking to make certain that Apache had trotted on to take shelter behind the biggest rocks, to the west. He had. Slocum waited.

After five minutes had passed, he was about to give up. Maybe he'd lucked out and hit the shooter with his first bullet. He hoped so. There was a long list of people who might have fired on him, but only one he figured to be in the immediate vicinity: Diego Vega. Vega had been on his trail since before he left California, although Slocum wasn't certain why he was so damned dogged about it. Sure, Slocum had turned his brother, Juan Vega, over to the authorities back in Big Mesa, but he would have been well within his rights to shoot him first.

The poster had said "Dead or Alive," after all.

Slocum figured Diego should have been grateful for that small favor.

It seemed Diego thought otherwise, though, and just as Slocum was about to stand up, Diego fired again, this time hitting the rock to Slocum's right with a sharp *pop* and a little spray of sparks and rock chips. Slocum, who had hit the ground the second he heard the shot being fired, caught the little pyrotechnic display out of the corner of his eye and thought, *Ain't he ever gonna get that gun fixed?* It had been firing high and to the right—well, that'd be Diego's left—ever since Campo Verde, the site of Slocum's last run-in with him.

Diego fired again, once again hitting the same rock with the same aftereffects, but this time, Slocum immediately fired up toward the source of the bullets. He let go five shots in rapid succession, which he doubted would hit anything but rock or brush, and was surprised when one shot—he couldn't be certain which—sent up a distant spray of blood.

It wasn't much, just enough to spatter the brush and cactus in the immediate area. But it was enough to convince Slocum that at least one of his slugs had hit the target.

Hunched behind the rocks, he waited a few minutes, but no more shots came his way. When he figured that Diego was either dead or incapable of firing, he slowly stood up and whistled softly to Apache, then swung up into the saddle.

"I might be wrong, but I think we'd best check on our old pal," he said as he urged the horse around the boulders and across the shallow ravine. Once he was on the other side and had climbed up to the place the shots had come from, he found what he was expecting: Diego lay dead, crumpled behind the scrub and rocks. One of Slocum's slugs had hit him in the center of his forehead—the kill shot—and an earlier slug had taken him high in the shoulder. Probably the reason for the blood spatter.

Slocum found Diego's horse and slung Diego's body across the saddle, securing it with the saddle's latigos. He figured that if he'd dropped off Juan with the authorities, he might as well do the same with Diego. There was a reward, after all.

Also, he knew they were only about an hour outside of Prescott. If a man couldn't drop a body off at the territorial capital's sheriff's office—and get paid for it, quick—where else could he drop it?

Slocum put a loop around Diego's pinto's neck, let out about a dozen feet of slack, then secured the other end to his saddle horn. He stepped up on Apache. "Let's go," he muttered, and Apache moved out. The pinto bearing Diego's body trailed along behind him.

By the time Slocum had delivered Diego's body, filled out the paperwork at the sheriff's office, and gotten his voucher, it was dark and the bank was closed. He'd have to cash in his voucher in the morning.

Untroubled by the prospect of having a night to kill in Prescott, he rode out to Whiskey Row, stabled Apache, and found himself a room at the Select Hotel. After he freshened up, he set out to find himself a drink or two, as well as a woman to share the libation. And a little something else he had in mind.

He walked down to the Blue Burro, a bar he'd frequented on a stopover here before, and took a seat at a corner table in the back. The saloon was just as noisy and smoke-filled as he remembered, the whiskey just as weak, and the girls just as pretty. Once you got a couple of shots in you, anyhow.

He had just tossed back his third—and ordered a beer—when a little blond thing sashayed over and sank herself into his lap. She couldn't have been older than fourteen, and he helped her right back up again.

"Sorry, miss," he said, tipping his hat, "but I believe you got me confused with somebody else." *Like, for instance, somebody who's into diddling kiddies,* he thought, disgusted. He'd heard stories of men like that, and personally, he thought they ought to be put away. Or strung up. He didn't much care which one, either.

The girl shrugged her shoulders and started to turn away, but he said, "Wait."

She turned back toward him, a glimmer of hope in her big blue eyes. She smiled a little.

Slocum pulled out his wallet and pulled two hundred dollars out of it, then handed it to the girl. It wasn't much to him, right now, but it'd mean the world to her. She accepted it, openmouthed, then stood there, staring at him.

Finally, she began, "Whatever you're wantin' me to do that costs this much, mister, I don't think I . . ."

Slocum shook his head. "I want you to go get yourself somethin' to eat. You're looking like you're starved half to death. And then I want you to gather up your belongin's and arrange to take the first stage out of town. And once you come to a nice place to live, I want you to find a real job. Not whorin'. All right?"

She blinked rapidly. And just stood there.

Finally, Slocum sat forward. "Go on, git," he said, motioning with his hand.

A wide smile of gratitude overtook her countenance.

"Thank you. Thank you ever so much, mister," she said before she turned and fairly scampered out the door.

Slocum grinned and shook his head before he picked up his beer and took a long drag on it. Seeing the look on her face: that had felt good. He hoped for the best for her. It sure couldn't get much worse than what she'd been living with.

"Now, what'd you do to make her spring-foot it out of here so cheery?" asked a new voice, female and decidedly more mature. He looked toward it and saw the speaker approaching his table. She was a deep brunette with green eyes and fair skin—probably as Irish as he was—and he guessed her age as about twenty-four: that was a little more like it, if you asked him.

He smiled at her and pulled out the chair next to his. "Have yourself a seat, honey."

She slid into it like a cat sliding into a pillow sling, propped her chin in her hands and her elbows on the table, and said, "Hi. My name's Tansy. Don't believe I seen you around here before, handsome."

The battle-scarred Slocum gave a good-natured little snort before he said, "Name's Slocum, and I been in this place once before, 'bout six or seven months back. Ain't surprised you don't remember me."

Her eyes were smiling, but they narrowed a bit, and Slocum knew she was ready to get down to business. She began, "What're you in the mood for, Slocum? Do you like it slow and lazy? Hot and fiery and frenzied-like? Do you—"

"As I live and breathe! Is that you, Slocum?" boomed a voice from across the room, and Slocum knew the speaker before he saw his face.

Slocum looked toward the source of the voice and

grinning wide, said, "Will Hutchins! What brings you to Prescott?"

Will winnowed his way through the crowd and appeared at Slocum's table. "Hey, Tansy," he said, without looking her way. Then he pulled out a chair, slapped Slocum on his shoulder, and said, "I live here now! Over on Fourth. Can you believe it? I'm a property owner and an upstanding citizen!"

"Who spends his evenings on Whiskey Row," Slocum said, then laughed out loud. The last time he'd seen Will, they were both gunning it out with a bunch of Mexican banditos—or Federales, he never knew which—down across the border, in Mexico.

"Damn right," said Will, before he craned his head back toward the bar and hollered, "Whiskey, Sam!" He shook his head, thick with blond hair, sneezed into a blue bandana he'd been carrying, and wiped his nose before he turned back to Slocum. "Goddamn it! How you been, Slocum?"

Slocum nodded, grinning. "All right, Will. Just fine, as a matter of fact. Came to town to collect a bounty on Diego Vega. Turned his brother, Juan, in to the sheriff over in California, and Diego'd been followin' me like a pup gone rabid ever since."

"Probably like a crazy pup gone rabid," Will said as a new girl slid his whiskey in front of him. Will's eyes were on the drink, but Slocum saw the girl shoot a sidelong glance at Tansy, who gave a quick shake of her head. This, apparently, was her territory and she wasn't about to share with anybody.

"Those Vega boys always was one looney pair of owlhoots," Will went on, after he'd had the first gulp of his whiskey. "I shoulda said the good stuff," he muttered, then tipped his head toward Tansy. "Sorry. Am I breakin' in on somethin'?"

Slocum chuckled. Same old Will—always too little, too late. But he said, "Nope. We were just conversin', weren't we, Tansy?"

Tansy took the hint and stood up. "Yeah. That's right. You want me, you know where to find me, Slocum."

As she moved off into the crowd, Will said, "Got some news the other day, Slocum. Somethin' you might be interested in."

Slocum took a swallow of beer, then arched a brow. "What's that?"

Will put his elbows on the table and leaned toward him. "The Dugan gang—all four of 'em—escaped custody three days back, down south of here. They was bein' transported down to the Territorial Prison. Killed the driver and the marshal and took off with the horses. Ranch hand out lookin' for strays found the bodies and what was left of the prison wagon."

Slocum's eyes narrowed. "Where, exactly?"

"They started from Phoenix goin' toward Yuma, and they'd been travelin' two days. That's all I know." Will tossed back the last of his whiskey before he added, "Been thinkin' 'bout goin' after 'em. Just been searchin' around for the right company." He stared into Slocum's eyes.

Slocum paused a moment, then asked, "What's the bounty, Will?" He knew Will wouldn't take to the trails again unless it was worth it. He'd always said that once he quit, that was it, period. But obviously, something had turned that period into a comma.

Lowering his voice again, Will said, "Twenty grand for all four. Ten for just Dugan, ten for the other three."

"Dead or alive, I take it."

A smile tickled at the corners of Will's mouth. "Yeah."

Slocum drained the last of his beer. He could always use half of twenty grand, but he was tired, and so was Apache. They could both use a good night's sleep. "We leave in the morning?"

Will grinned. "Fine by me."

2

The next morning, Slocum and his pal Will Hutchins set out from Prescott at about eight. Will had shown up around seven, but Slocum insisted on having breakfast at the café first. It was a good idea. He was sick of his own cooking, and he knew from sad experience that Will was a total washout in the culinary department. He had a steak with pan fries, four eggs over easy with a half pound of bacon, three cups of coffee, and a slab of apple pie with cheddar.

"You fattenin' up for the winter?" Will, picking at his own toast and eggs, asked him.

"Wrong time a' year," Slocum answered, around a mouthful of steak.

And that was the sum total of their breakfast conversation. In silence, they retrieved Slocum's horse, Apache, and Slocum let Will lead the way on his blue roan, Duster. Duster was new, at least to Slocum. Will's last mount—anyway, the one he'd ridden when Slocum knew him—had been a palomino gelding called Pyrite,

9

Pye for short. He made the mistake of asking Will about him.

"Got shot out from under me up in Utah," Will replied. "It was Johnny Wade Cummings who done it, the son of a bitch. Didn't even kill him all the way. He left that for me to take care of."

"Sorry," Slocum muttered. He really was, too. Pye had been a good horse, and Slocum knew how hard it was to put down a good one. Even a bad one, for that matter.

After a while, it became apparent that somebody should have shot Will. He just wouldn't shut up. He talked about everything, except anything that might have mattered to their current project. After a while, Slocum just let the words bubble over him while he settled into his own thoughts, which were currently centered on Bronc Dugan and his boys.

He figured that Bronc had likely headed south, for the border. Slocum would have, if their positions had been reversed. Then again, he never would have been in Bronc Dugan's position: sentenced to hang for not just one, but four murders. The Territory had been so mad at him that they'd taken the trouble to transport him down to the Territorial Prison and do it up right. Or tried to.

Right, Slocum thought, snorting softly. *Like their rope is better.* It all came from the same hemp fields, so far as he was concerned.

Anyhow, they had only swiped the two horses that were pulling the wagon. They'd need to pick up a couple more. Monkey Springs was probably where they'd stop. It was close, and on their route.

He wondered about the three who were running with Dugan these days. Slocum had had the misfortune of crossing Dugan's path back in the days when he was hustling silver miners up in Colorado. He'd already killed at least six men back then, and at best, he was a nasty piece of business. In those days Dugan ran with the Miller boys, Chad and Tom, plus Tony Ortiz and Finn Hannigan. The Millers, Ortiz, and Hannigan were all long dead, as were countless others of Dugan's sidekicks, but Dugan had just kept on. Until he got caught and convicted this last time, that is.

You couldn't keep a rotten egg down, Slocum guessed. Well, *they* couldn't. He had every intention of giving Dugan his just deserts.

In spades.

At around noon, Slocum's stomach started to growl. At around one, he said, "Let's stop and eat somethin', Will. I'm starvin'. 'Sides," he added, "the horses need to rest."

He must have let some of his cranky out when he said it, because Will reined in, swiveled back in the saddle, and said, "I asked you an hour ago if you was peckish, and you didn't answer."

"Sorry." Slocum swung down out of the saddle. "Guess I didn't hear you."

Will dismounted, as well. He didn't look too happy.

Slocum ignored him and got busy with his saddlebags. It was a long way down to Monkey Springs, or wherever Will was leading him. He ripped a hunk of jerky off the chuck he'd got in town, and began to gnaw on it.

"No fire?" Will asked.

"No time," came Slocum's reply. He swallowed his first bite of jerky and washed it down with canteen water before he added, "I take it we're headed for Monkey Springs?"

Will leaned an elbow against his horse's saddle and said, "So you were listenin', after all."

Slocum hadn't been, but he smiled a little and gnawed another bite of jerky off his hunk.

Thankfully, Will finished his own lunch in silence, then wandered off, probably to take a leak. Once he put the jerky away, Slocum watered the horses, then took himself a long piss. Will came walking back while Slocum was lighting a quirley, nodded at him, and swung up on his horse.

Slocum asked, "You ready?"

Will gave him a sidelong look.

"I watered your horse, in case you're interested."

Will grunted then moved out.

Slocum shrugged, threw his leg over Apache, and goosed him into a jog to catch up.

He was even with Will in no time, and dropped back down into a walk. "So, you figure they're headin' south, too."

Will nodded.

Slocum's brow furrowed. "Y'know, you're awful quiet for somebody who talked his jaws off all morning."

Will poked a finger at his own neck and wiggled it. "Sore throat," he rasped, then coughed.

Slocum held back a laugh. At least it'd keep Will quiet for the afternoon ride. He said, "Well, best to rest it for the afternoon, right?" When Will nodded, Slocum said, "I know a shortcut that'll save us a few miles and get us out of the Bradshaws quicker. C'mon."

Slocum turned toward the southeast, and once he was certain Will was following—and the trail allowed—he pushed Apache into a soft lope. This trip was going to take long enough without walking all the damn way there!

* * *

Over the next few days—the time it took to get them completely out on the flat and well on their way to Monkey Springs—the two had managed to come to a meeting point on the conversation. Which meant that Will talked only when Slocum asked him a question, or when he had something really important to say. For instance, "Watch out! Rattler!" fell into the latter category.

As far as Slocum was concerned, he only talked when he felt like it, which meant rarely, if ever. Will got used to the new situation fairly quickly, and actually slid into the new routine like a forgotten, then re-found, pair of friendly old boots. These two had ridden together before, after all, and quite pleasantly. It just took Will a day or so to remember how.

They rode into Monkey Springs—a town not much more than a wide spot in the road, if there had been a road to begin with—and headed straight for the sheriff's office. Turned out, after not some little searching, that it was hidden away in a back room at the town mercantile.

The store owner, who had introduced himself as "Jennings" on the way in, said his second words just as Slocum raised his knuckles to knock on the sheriff's door.

"Ain't there," said the storekeep.

"Where is he, then?" asked Slocum.

Jennings nodded at the saloon across the street. "Might not be too drunk to talk to, this early in the day."

Slocum nodded, and Will touched his hat's brim and said, "Appreciate it, Jennings," as they left the store.

They crossed what passed for a road and entered the saloon. Well, Slocum figured you could almost call it a saloon, anyhow. The place was only ten or twelve feet wide and maybe fifteen feet long, with a manned bar running down one twelve-foot wall and, in lieu of tables, another bar, set flush against the wall opposite and running down its length. There wasn't a chair in the place, just ten or fifteen bar stools.

"What can I get for you gents?" the barkeep asked as they pushed through the batwing doors.

Will spoke up first. "Town sheriff?"

The bartender nodded down to the farthest end of the bar, and the lone customer. "There he sits. Sheriff Jack O'Casey, such as he is."

Slocum said, "Thanks," then added, "Two beers. We'll take 'em down to the end, there." He indicated Sheriff O'Casey's location, then muttered, "C'mon," to Will.

They walked between the patronless bars, skirting stray stools as they went. Will scooted a few back into place. When they reached the sheriff, Slocum pulled out a stool on the far side of him, Will on the near.

"Jack O'Casey?" said Slocum.

O'Casey looked up, a little bleary-eyed, and nodded. He began, "Who—?"

Slocum stuck out his hand. "Name's Slocum, John Slocum, and that feller on your other side is Will Hutchins, late of the U.S. marshal's office. We're down here lookin' for some escapees—Bronc Dugan and his bunch. They come through here?"

Sheriff O'Casey muttered, "Dugan?"

Will tried. He pounded on O'Casey's shoulder until he got the sheriff's attention, then tried asking him again.

The bartender showed up with their beers. "You askin' about Bronc Dugan and his gang?"

Both Slocum and Will nodded—Slocum somewhat warily.

The bartender added, "Then you oughta be askin' somebody who's got his wits about him at least half the time."

Will said, "Like you, for instance?"

"Like me," the bartender said. "And call me Gary. Garrison Douglas is the whole of it."

Will shook his hand. Slocum took a draw on his beer. It had been a long and thirsty ride this morning.

"They was in here three, mayhap four days ago," Gary went on. "They was four of 'em altogether, and they didn't drink nothin' but beer. No offense."

Will said, "None taken. What else?"

"Those sonsabitches stole my horse, that's what else!" Gary yelped, and slapped the bar top with his rag. "I want my goddamn horse back! I want somebody to do somethin' about it!"

Sheriff O'Casey muttered, "Want mine back, too, Gary," before his head collapsed down in his pillowing arms. "Somebody get my Daisy home," he breathed before he passed out.

"That's two," Will said to Slocum.

"Oh, I ain't done yet," Gary said casually, and both Slocum and Will leaned in.

3

"They come dragglin' in here, two to a horse and looking like a hunnert and twenty miles a' bad road," Gary went on. "Didn't even have no tack on them horses. Looked to me like they started off with a wagon or somethin', mebbe busted an axle and had to make do."

Slocum broke in, "Did you ask?"

"Nope," Gary said with a shake of his head. "Didn't seem the sort to be asked questions. Seemed real rough, all of 'em." He gave a scratch to his stubbly neck. "Anyhow, they come here first to get their whistles wet. Had several beers each, they did, and then two of 'em left. Other two stayed and had lunch. We had roast beef for sandwiches that day." He paused, pursing his lips. "Musta been four days back that they was in, then, not three. Been outta beef four days, 'cause they et up the last of it."

Will coaxed, "So two of 'em left, you say? Where'd they take off to?"

"Well, we found that out later, didn't we?" Gary snapped.

"Sorry," said Will, holding up his hands. "Tell it your way, then. Don't mind me."

Still visibly annoyed, Gary turned toward Slocum and continued, "Anyhow . . ." He glanced back toward Will, who raised his brows and wiggled both hands innocently. "So anyhow," Gary began again, "'bout the time the first two finished their lunch, the two that had been gone come back. The four of 'em sat there for a while, talkin' over somethin' or other, then the pair what had already had lunch took off, and the second two had them some lunch. Same stuff. Roast beef sandwiches. And tater salad. Mandy—she's the storekeeper's wife—she makes a good tater salad."

"That's real interestin', Gary, but—" Will interrupted, then clammed up right away, once both Gary and Slocum shot him warning looks. Gary apparently wanted to tell the story his way, and Slocum was determined to let him. He wanted every detail he could get, even if most of it proved to be worthless.

Will and Slocum were in that bar for a good hour and a half, going through beer after beer, and when they were finished listening to Gary's story—and Gary had finished telling it—Slocum boiled it down.

All four had come into the bar. Soon after, two men left, leaving Dugan and the fourth man to eat lunch. Apparently, the first two men to leave were scouting out the horse situation, and managed to spot what they were going to rustle when they left.

It seemed that they came back happy, and settled down to a meal while Dugan and the other man took off for parts unknown. This later turned out to be the general store, where they made off with two handguns, ammunition, and provisions, and left the storekeeper bound, gagged, and locked up in the sheriff's office. Gary also told them (at great length) that they made off as well with a big sack full of penny candy, so Slocum figured at least one of the four to have a powerful sweet tooth.

When those two came back, Dugan—the only one who'd dropped his name to Gary—paid the tab for all four men, and they left. They then proceeded down the way a bit to the livery, where they made off with four horses, plus the tack for each, plus feed. They left the horses on which they'd ridden into town tied to the rail out front of the saloon.

And the sheriff, as he had today, had slept through the entire event, draped across the bar.

Slocum figured it was the only thing that had saved his life.

From Gary, he got a good description of all four men and all four stolen horses, which Will wrote down on a small tablet of paper he pulled from his pocket.

Gary also told him that the Dugan gang had ridden off to the south, something Slocum had already figured. Where else was left for them to head? It seemed that Dugan had run himself out of other possibilities.

Once Slocum and Will had paid their tab at the saloon, they moseyed out of town, to the south. Slocum tried to pick up Dugan's tracks, but had no luck until they were a half mile out of town. Gradually, as cart horses and saddle mounts alike turned off the main path, he made out the tracks of four different horses, all following along in a line. Headed south.

He called back over his shoulder, "Got 'em."

"Me, too," came Will's reply. He trotted up to ride beside Slocum. "Least, I got four. Same as you?"

Slocum pointed ahead and down at the broken brush, and the faint trail obvious only to the well-trained eye.

Will studied the ground for a second. "Yup. Same ones."

Slocum allowed himself half a smile. Will was good. Always had been, always would be. Well, aside from the talking.

Now that they both had an eye for the trail, Slocum nudged Apache up into a soft lope. Will took the cue and followed along. They rode on opposite sides of the Dugan gang's path, Slocum to the right and Will to the left, and Slocum figured if they kept this up, they might run across the gang tomorrow, mid-morning.

On the other hand, he hadn't counted on Will's horse, Duster, throwing a shoe that afternoon.

Will was walking with his nose to the ground, going back over his own tracks, trying to find the missing shoe. "Goddamn it!" he hollered as he peered beneath a new patch of manzanita. Then "Son of a bitch!" as he walked to the next patch of scrubby foliage.

To the tune of Will's entire vocabulary of cuss words (including a few that even Slocum hadn't heard), Slocum stepped back up on Apache and, leading Duster, began to amble back the way he'd come. For all of Will's griping, he was looking in the wrong place. Slocum figured that Duster's shoe had probably flown off to the left, maybe twenty or more feet. They'd been traveling at a pretty sharp clip.

He saw it when he was halfway caught up to Will, and he hollered, "Got your shoe!" before he dropped Duster's reins, ground-tying him, and Will came trotting over. Just like Slocum had figured, it was off to the left, although not quite so far. Maybe fifteen feet instead of twenty. It'd been a pretty good guess, though.

He leaned over and snatched it up without dismounting, and turned it in his hand. Without a word, Will stopped dead in his tracks, then turned around and went back to his horse.

Slocum could fix this. He already knew that Duster's hoof wall wasn't damaged—that was the most important part—and he still had nails, both a few left in the shoe and some spares in his saddlebags.

He rode back over to where Duster patiently waited—and Will, not so patiently. He climbed down off Apache again, unbuckled his saddlebag, and began to feel around for the tools he'd need.

Will came up behind him. "Where the hell was it?" he demanded.

Slocum tipped his head back. "Over there, in the sage."

"I wasn't ridin' over there, I was ridin' over here!"

Slocum let out a little sigh. "He threw it over that way. You knew he doesn't travel four-square, didn't you?"

Will snorted. "Course I knew! But that's still too far for him to throw a shoe, even at a lope."

"Well, you and him argue about it. Me, I'm gonna get this shoe back on before he decides to go lame on you." Slocum had located some nails, his rasp, a hammer, and a pair of nippers, just in case, and with the old shoe slung over one wrist, he walked to where Duster stood.

Will was at Duster's head. "Way the hell over there!" Slocum heard him mutter. "How the hell'd you do that?"

Slocum wished he'd swear some more. It was kind of entertaining. But he leaned into Duster, then pulled up his hind hoof. "You're a lucky man, Will," he said after he'd inspected the hoof, inside and out.

"Bad luck, mebbe," Will growled.

"No, good luck, on account of he didn't tear up his hoof any. Nails must've pulled clean out."

Will grunted, deep in his throat.

Slocum ignored him and got down to business. Duster was calm and didn't give him any trouble, and it looked to him as if the shoe hadn't been nailed on right in the first place, as if the ends of the nails hadn't been bent over, just clipped off even with the outside wall of the hoof. He did the job right this time, and finished up pretty damn certain that Duster wouldn't be throwing that shoe again anytime soon.

While he put his tools back into his saddlebag, Will, who had been staring at Duster, said, "You could always be a farrier, Slocum."

Slocum took this as a compliment, but said, "Never seen myself as a blacksmith. I'm just a patch-up man."

"Whatever. Nice job, though."

"Thanks." Slocum rebuckled his saddlebag and stepped up on Apache. "You comin'?"

Will looked up from his horse's hoof. "What? Oh, yeah."

He mounted, and the two men set out, back on the trail. Slocum wondered, a little late, if Will'd had the horse shod all the way around by the same smithy at the same time. If so, they were likely in for more trouble. But since they'd already moved up into a lope, he didn't ask. He'd wait until they stopped for the night, then check the horse out.

Will looked happy as a clam, though. Slocum was just happy that Will was a competent enough horseman that he was sufficiently in tune with Duster to know when the horse wasn't traveling right—which he wouldn't have been after he threw that shoe. It took an experienced rider—and one who really knew his mount—

to notice something like that, particularly when the horse wasn't limping, wasn't even favoring the leg.

That evening, they camped a few miles before they came to the low, dusty, southern hills that bounded the U.S. and Mexico. They had stopped near what Slocum knew to be the last water until they came into Mexico, if they kept to their current path. They stocked up, even getting out Slocum's canvas water bags. Those, they'd fill in the morning. The canvases would hold far, far more than their canteens, and would sweat, keeping the water cool for themselves and their horses.

Slocum knew those hills. He knew how good that cool water would taste when they were deep into the hard country, without even a barrel cactus to grant them some moisture.

Will was building a fire, and had the coffeepot ready to put on it. He also had the rabbits that he'd shot earlier skinned and spitted, waiting for the flames. While he prodded the fire, Slocum took the time to check Duster's hooves. He had just put down the last one when Will called, "Whatcha doin', Slocum?"

Slocum walked back to the fire and explained his search. "Whoever put on that off hind shoe? I wouldn't go back to him again."

Will shook his head in disgust. "And you say the other three look fine?"

Slocum said, "Far's I can tell."

Will's head was still shaking. "Last time I ever try to shoe my own horse," he grumbled.

Slocum burst out laughing. "You did that botched job yourself? On purpose?"

"Yes, on purpose," Will shot back angrily.

Slocum tried to control his laughter. "Sorry, Will. It's

just that anybody who's been around horses as long as you oughta know—"

"Shut up!"

Slocum, knowing he was going to have to ride with Will for a good patch longer—and also not wishing to permanently anger his friend—said no more, except "Sorry."

Will busied himself making biscuits and tending the roasting rabbits. Slocum rolled a couple of quirleys as slowly as possible, keeping one eye on Will the whole time. Eventually, Will's mood seemed to lighten, and Slocum stopped watching him. Will was a good man and a great one at times, but he had a problem handling his anger. On rare occasions, Slocum had seen him do quite a bit of damage. In this case, he was definitely the man for the task, though. He'd confided to Slocum that the Dugan boys had done an ugly job on the marshal and guard that were with them. One had been crucified upside down on the jail wagon.

"Slocum?"

It startled him, lost as he was in trying to picture that poor man's death, and he let out an embarrassed snort, followed by a somber "Yeah, Will?"

"Chow's ready."

Breathing a sigh of relief, Slocum took the plate Will held toward him. "Thanks," he said, and leaned back. He picked up his fork. "Looks good!" It did, too.

Will gave him a quick smile. "Yeah, them rabbits browned up nice, didn't they?"

4

The next morning, after they broke camp and filled the water bags, they set out toward the south and the sandy hills on the horizon.

Apache was a little jumpy, which surprised Slocum. He was usually a steady horse, despite his wild coloring. Bright sorrel with a long blanket of white, covered in fist-sized Appaloosa spots, he was a horse you didn't soon forget.

Not by Slocum, anyhow. He'd bought him from a rancher up in Palouse country, a rancher who didn't know what he had. Apache took to training like a duck took to water, and Slocum had him schooled in the basics inside a month. Six weeks later, Slocum found out that the gelding had cow sense as well. While he was riding south through California, he'd come across a small herd of cattle and decided to try to cut a bald-faced calf from the herd.

The calf resisted the process, but in less than five minutes, Apache had figured out what he was supposed to do and was pouncing left, then right, then left again to keep that calf separated from the herd.

Slocum smiled just thinking about it.

But this morning, the gelding just wasn't right. It was as if he smelled smoke or something, but there was nothing ablaze, and no other threat that Slocum could see or sense. Once again, he stroked the Appy's neck to soothe him. "Easy, Apache," he said soothingly. "There's nothin' here to be afraid of."

Nothin' yet, anyway, he thought to himself. Bronc Dugan and his bunch were up there someplace.

Big Tony, a mountain of a man and one of Bronc Dugan's current hangers-on, slid back down the sandy, gravelly hill on his belly, rolling over when he was halfway down. He climbed to his feet and turned to one of the mounted men waiting for him.

"Two riders," Big Tony said. "One's ridin' an Appaloosa."

"What's the other one ridin'?" Bronc Dugan asked.

Tony shrugged. "A horse. Blue roan, I think. Anybody we know?"

Dugan, a good-sized man with graying red hair and a ragged mustache, paused a moment before he said, "Don't ring a bell. But still, sounds like they're followin' our track. They ridin' nice horses?"

Tony nodded.

Dugan rumbled, "Prob'ly marshals, then."

Dave and Roy, the two other mounted men, and also brothers, sat back in their saddles. Dave, who was as dark-haired as his brother, clean-shaven, and the youngest of them all, said, "You reckon Roy could pick 'em off from here? He's a pretty fair marksman."

That was putting it mildly. Roy was a champion with

a rifle, having won several medals. However, he wasn't sure about moving targets that far back. He said, "Tony, were they camped where we was?"

Tony nodded. "Exact same place. Right near that little spring."

Roy shook his head. "Forget it. They're too far out for even me to hit."

Dave shook his head. "Roy, you're just bein' shy."

"The word you're lookin' for is humble," said Roy. "And no, I'm not. Pinky swear."

Tony, having put away his binoculars, clambered back up on his horse and turned toward Dugan expectantly, waiting for orders.

Dugan, lips pursed, stared at his hands, which were clasped on his saddle horn. Finally, he looked up and immediately reined his horse to the south. He looked at no man, only the territory ahead, when he said, "They're about a half day behind us, Big Tony?"

"Looks like," the big man replied.

"Then screw 'em. We're goin' to Mexico, and we'll be there before they catch up. U.S. marshals won't follow us over the border."

He took off at a lope, skirting the southern hill, then cutting up to the shallow valley between it and the next one.

Silently, obediently, the others followed him.

At noon, Slocum and Will stopped to rest the horses and grab themselves some lunch. They were just barely into the hills, having followed the gang's tracks up and through two little valleys in the range. Will had just finish peeing for the fourth time, and dipped into the water bag again.

Slocum chewed on a piece of hardtack. "You made

outta water these days, Will? You been pissin' up a storm ever since we left Prescott."

"I got me a straight pipe, all right," Will said. This time, he offered water to Duster before he looked for something to feed his face. Slocum had already offered water to Apache, who had drunk his full.

"Come on you sudden?"

Will shook his head. "Been gettin' worse over the last year or so." He turned toward Slocum. "You a doctor all of a sudden?"

"No. But I was just wonderin' if you'd seen one."

"Ain't none a' your business, far as I can see. But no, I ain't."

Slocum didn't respond. Will was right. It was none of his business, although he couldn't help worrying about it. He'd had an old friend, Soren was his name, who'd had the same sort of problem. Turned out he had a cancer, and was dead inside a couple months.

"Been thinkin' about seeing one, though," Will added, breaking the silence.

Slocum nodded. "Good. That's a good idea, Will."

"Mayhap after we take care a' these owlhoots and get back to Prescott."

"Good idea, Will," Slocum repeated. He dug out his jerky and tore off a corner of it. He wasn't much for sick people, didn't like thinking about the possibility of illness or death. He decided a change of subject was in order. He said, "I'm thinkin' we're about a half day behind 'em, now. What you think?"

Will was gnawing on something he'd pulled out of his saddlebag. Mouth full, he nodded his agreement.

Slocum took a drink from his canteen to wash down the jerky, then prepared to mount up again. "'Bout ready?" he asked.

Will swallowed, then nodded. He and Slocum swung up into their saddles at the same time.

"I'd like to catch up with the bastards before nightfall," Will said as they started out.

"Best kick it up a notch, then." Slocum urged Apache into a lope, and Will followed along.

They crossed over into Mexico at roughly four that afternoon, and continued to follow Dugan's trail. Slocum figured that Dugan couldn't be too awfully far ahead—the tracks the gang had laid down on the south side of the river were still damp, and things didn't stay damp too long in the Sonoran Desert.

"Best be on the lookout?" Will asked him as he mounted back up.

"Best be." Slocum looked ahead. It was flat for a few miles before the country got rough again, this time rising up in low rocks that eventually worked their way up into mountains, farther to the south. Slocum knew hard country when he saw it, let alone rode through it, and he'd be damned if he'd follow those boys that far.

Now, Will was dead-set on catching up to Dugan and his boys—and, Slocum thought, killing all four of them—before nightfall. Slocum figured somebody was going to get caught, all right, but what would they do with them next? And the whole thing was a dice roll. It looked like Dugan could be doing the deciding just as easily as could he and Will.

They rode on down to the south, ears and eyes open for any rustle, any flash that might give away their quarry's position. And Apache was still spooky. That bothered Slocum as much as anything else.

"Easy, boy," he cooed to the horse. "It's all right." But

he didn't mean it, and Apache knew. The horse still fretted, as he had all morning.

"You say something, pard?" Will said. They were riding even now, with Will casting his eyes to the east and Slocum to the west.

"Just talkin' to my horse," Slocum said.

Will nodded. "Antsy this mornin', ain't he?"

Slocum gave a quick nod. "Somethin's comin'."

Will knew. He said nothing.

Suddenly a strong wind blew up from the southeast, sharp and filled with biting sand. Slocum turned his head away and pulled his bandana up to cover his nose and mouth, while Will did the same. Apache lowered his head and tugged at the bit.

"Maybe this was it," Slocum said through his bandana, hoping for an excuse for the horse.

"You're prob'ly right," Will allowed, and Slocum noted that Will was almost shouting to be heard over the rising howl of the wind.

Visibility was suddenly cut in half, then half again. Slocum couldn't see the mountains rising to the south any longer, although he knew they were there. He shouted, "We're gonna lose the track!" and sank his heels into Apache.

Without a word, Will goosed Duster. They kept pace with Slocum, riding alongside him as the wind, ever changing directions, buffeted them from all sides.

In a low cave in the hills to the south, Bronc Dugan and his men had taken refuge from the storm. Dugan had gotten out his binoculars and moved to the mouth of the cave to try to see if they were being followed. But the wind had risen so much that he couldn't see more than a hundred feet, and he soon dropped the binoculars to dangle around his neck.

"Anything?" asked Roy, behind him in the cave. Farther inside, Dave was holding the horses.

"Nothin'," replied Dugan. "Nothin' but dirt and wind, damn it. Can't see more'n a hundred feet. I wish we were in Texas."

"George Collins'd be tickled to see you, I reckon," said Big Tony, who squatted against a cave's wall. He had taken off his hat, and his blond hair was the only light-colored point in the cave. The grit-filled wind blotted out the sun outside, allowing only the most feeble rays into the rocky hollow.

Dugan snorted derisively. "Yeah, him and a few others . . ."

Roy asked, "So what do we do now?"

Dugan walked back inside the cave and slid down the wall near Tony. "We wait," he said. "We wait it out."

5

Slocum couldn't fight the wind anymore.

Visibility was down to ten, maybe fifteen feet, and the wind showed no signs of abating. He took advantage of a large boulder on his right and shouted to Will to follow him.

The boulder did provide some relief from the biting wind, even more when he followed its edge farther south and found it was just the first in a line of big rocks he remembered seeing from the river's bank.

Good. He had a much better idea of where they were and how far they'd come. The mountains, or at least the beginnings of them, lay not far to the south.

He slid down off Apache, then pulled the bandana off his own face to wipe the horse's. Apache's nostrils were caked with damp sand, his eyes as well. "Been a rough day, buddy, ain't it?" Slocum said. Will stepped down off Duster and began to minister to his face, too.

In the shelter of the rocks, visibility was much better. Where Slocum's earlier view hadn't been clear much

31

farther out than the V between Apache's ears, from the protection of the boulders he could see out several feet. It wasn't much, but it was an improvement. He backed as far as he could into the crevice between two massive boulders, leading Apache, then grabbed his canteen and slid down to the ground.

His head hanging low, the horse looked as if he was damn glad to be out of the wind. Slocum couldn't blame him. Once he'd caught his breath and had a long drink of water, he forced himself up on his feet again to heft down the water bag. He filled his canteen again, then let Apache drink. From where he stood, he could see Will, his back turned as he pissed into the sand.

Only a moment after Slocum had loosened Apache's saddle and sat himself down, back in the protection of the crevice, he was joined by Will—and Will's Duster. Slocum wasn't exactly thrilled by this level of togetherness. Neither was Apache, who tried to bite Duster's neck.

"Hey!" shouted Will. He took a step toward Apache. "None a' that foolishness, now!"

Slocum raised a brow. Apache had been startled by Will, but that was all. Slocum had killed men for less, but right at the moment he was too tired—and Will too good a friend—for him to retaliate. He only said, "Easy there, Apache," and snapped the horse's reins lest he try to bite again.

Apache understood, and allowed Duster to walk up even with him and stop, their saddles brushing stirrup leathers. Apache wasn't very happy about it, though. He leaned away, to the side, and gave Slocum a look that said, *You're gonna pay for this later.*

Will slipped down the rock to crouch beside Slocum. "Where the Sam Hill'd this crap come from?" He waved his hand upward as he shouted over the whistle and howl of the wind.

Slocum shrugged. "Happens from time to time. Guess this time we just rolled boxcars."

"Hell, we could be holed up twenty feet from 'em and not know it," Will grumbled.

"Thought of that already." Slocum had, too. It was why he'd investigated the rocks farther south—about twenty feet south, anyway—before he came back here and settled in. "I checked. We're safe."

Will rubbed the grime from his forehead. "Don't know whether to be happy about that or pissed."

"Know what you mean."

"Don't know about you, ol' buddy," said Will, shaking out his bandana, "but I ain't ready for supper yet. More like I'm ready for a nap."

"Suit yourself," Slocum said. "In fact, think a little snooze would do me good, too."

Both men looped their reins around their wrists and pulled down the rims of their hats. Will was asleep almost immediately. Slocum stayed awake long enough to tell Apache, "I'm only closin' my eyes, big feller. You keep your teeth to yourself, all right?"

The sun was just setting when Slocum awoke, the dimness of light due only to a sinking sun and not to the dust storm, which had moved on about an hour ago. He stood up, his back still against the rock, then moved forward, backing Apache out of his way. He wanted a good look down the way before it got too dark to see anything at all.

When he got outside, he was pleased to find that the view was darkening, but clear. It looked as though rain was moving in from the west, as well. Nights like this were rare, but he couldn't count how many he'd spent out here with weather just like this. He knew that the wind would blow up like a silverback grizzly on a tear, and the rain would come pelting in on an angle. He'd best find them a cave to hunker in, and one of those would most likely be down in the mountains.

He said, "Will? You awake?"

Some grumbling came from back in the crevice, and then Will stuck his head out. "What you want, Slocum?" Then he lifted his eyes. "Hey! The wind's gone!"

Slocum was tightening Apache's girth strap. "We'd best find a cave for the night, or at least some place with a good overhang. It's gonna get mighty windy and mighty wet. Chilly, too."

Will nodded. "Check." He tightened Duster's saddle, as well. "Gonna be one bitch of a blowup?"

"You've got it."

"Hope we can get a cave, then. A nice deep one."

Slocum nodded against the wind, which was just starting to come up again and was threatening to take his hat to El Paso. He crammed it down firmly and swung up into the saddle. Will was right behind him, so he started the ride down toward the mountains. There was still no sign of Bronc Dugan or his boys.

But after Slocum had ridden about fifteen or twenty minutes, some of those at an easy jog, he saw something over on his right and up ahead that made him rein in Apache. Will saw it, too.

"Is that a fire goin', back inside?" he asked.

Slocum nodded. He said, "Looks like we found our boys."

"Well, c'mon! Let's get 'em!" Will said.

But Slocum had different plans. He grabbed Will's reins before he could take off, and said, "Wait."

"Wait for what? Wait for them to see us and get off the first shot?"

Slocum shook his head. "No. Wait for the storm to come up so we can get past 'em."

"Oh, fine. Then we'll be the ones soaked and spendin' the night in some cold cave!"

"Maybe. Or maybe we'll be the ones to take 'em by surprise when they're ridin' down the canyon come mornin'," Slocum said. "See?"

Will snorted, but he said, "Fine. Just fine," and slipped off Duster. He led the horse back against the rocks, grumbling the whole way.

Slocum followed him. There was no way he was going to ride up in there, two against four, in crystal weather. Not and expect to come out in one piece, anyway.

Tucked back into the rocks, he said, "What you got against Bronc Dugan, anyhow? With you wantin' to charge in there and kill anything that moves, I'm thinkin' it's personal." Actually, he'd been wondering since the beginning.

Will pursed his lips for a moment, then said, "He killed my partner, all right? It was after they robbed the bank at Gunderson, up Colorado way. We was trailin' 'em, givin' chase, and they picked him off from up in the rocks somewhere. Ted Holder was my partner's name. He was a real good man, left a widow and three kids behind."

Slocum said, "I didn't know. I'm sorry, Will. Sorry for your loss."

"Thanks," Will replied. "I was with the marshal's office then, and they decided to let 'em ride free till the next time, seein' as how we'd lost so many men already." He took a deep breath, then added, "It's why I quit."

Slocum nodded. "Been wonderin' why, but I didn't want to ask. I figured it musta been somethin' tough."

"Tough is right. And someday, if I ever get a chance, I'm gonna put paid to that damn head marshal that called a halt to the whole thing, too."

It began to rain, just like that. And it was no ordinary rain. It came in almost horizontally, in driving sheets. Slocum glanced up. The sky had gone from black to yellow, filled with clouds broken only by the dim, filtered glow of the moon.

He said, "My pappy used to call storms like this goose-drownders."

Will let loose the tiniest of smiles. "My pa—that was Big Will—used to call 'em turd-floaters."

Slocum chuckled, and Will joined in.

Then Slocum said, "Let's cut across the canyon, get behind those big rocks. Bet we won't have to go far before we find us a hidey-hole."

Will nodded. "Gotcha," he said, and mounted up.

Unaware of the two men crossing the canyon mere yards away from their cave's opening, Dugan's men were building up their fire and trying to cook dinner. Dugan didn't feel all that hungry. He was just anxious for that first cup of hot coffee. The weather had grown chilly about the same time the rain rolled in, and his bones weren't used to it. Somehow, he'd had the idea that once he crossed the border he'd never be cold again.

Well, so much for that. Here it was, his first night in Mexico, and he was freezing his tail off.

Big Tony had just set the pot on, and Roy and Dave were slicing ham for the skillet.

"Somebody gonna cook us up some biscuits?" Dugan

asked. The sight of that meat had him hungering for a
ham sandwich all of a sudden.

"Gonna stir some up once the ham's on," Roy replied.

Dave looked up, focusing on the rugged wall behind
his brother's back. "Roy?" he said, lifting a hand to point.
"'Nother scorpion."

"Aw, crud," Roy muttered, and swatted it with the
side of his knife blade, then flicked its corpse to the
back of the cave with the blade's point. "They shouldn't
call this country Mexico, 'less Mex is Spanish for scorpion."

Dave chuckled, and Big Tony said, "Mebbe we should
change it to 'Scorpico,' then."

"Hey, that's good," said Roy with a laugh.

Annoyed, Dugan said, "You boys wanna get onto
them biscuits?"

"Sure, Bronc," Roy said. He wiped his knife blade on
his pants before he dragged over the possibles bag and
began to search for the flour, salt, soda, and eggs. "Doin'
it right now."

Dugan grunted. He glanced outside and shook his
head. Somebody could have driven a team of Clydes-
dales down the gorge and he wouldn't have seen it. It
was a mean bastard of a rain, coming fast and hard, and
it was filled with bits of desert landscape—sand, gravel,
small clumps of cactus, and thorny twigs—it had picked
up on its way east.

He heard the ham beginning to sizzle, and turned back
toward the fire in time to see Roy set the Dutch oven—
filled, he assumed, with biscuits—over the flames.

His stomach rumbled.

He guessed he'd been hungry all along and was just
too nerved up to notice. But he could already taste those

ham sandwiches now. "Coffee ready?" he asked Big Tony.

Tony eyed the pot. "Few more minutes, Boss."

Dugan nodded. "Let me know," he said, crossing his arms.

His eyes drifted closed.

6

The morning dawned, brisk and clear, to find Slocum already awake and gazing out over the canyon floor from behind a cluster of boulders. In fact, he'd awakened at some time around four. Will dozed behind him, hunkered next to a wall that granted him scarce protection from last night's rain. But it was something. With the hills above shading them, neither had begun to dry out yet, and Slocum shivered.

But the sun shone brightly into the cave where Dugan and his boys had taken shelter. Slocum figured it wouldn't be long before they stuck their heads out like turkeys at a Thanksgiving shoot.

He didn't want to start firing right off, though. He wanted to see all four owlhoots outside their cave where he could get off a clean shot or two before they scrambled for cover again.

He took a step back and stuck his leg out, prodding Will with the toe of his boot. Will opened one cranky eye and glared at him.

"Rise and shine, pretty boy," Slocum said.

"Pretty boy, my ass," Will grumbled as he sat forward and stretched his arms to loosen the joints. "My ma was afeared to take me out in public till I was three, I was such a butt-ugly little shaver!"

"Stop braggin'," said Slocum as he moved back to peer back up the canyon, over the rocks. No movement, yet.

"No brag, just truth, plain and simple," Will said as he stood—somewhat creakily—and moved next to Slocum to peer over the boulders. "Anything yet?"

"Nothin'," Slocum replied. "But sooner or later, they gotta come out."

"I hear Santa Anna said the same thing at the Alamo."

"Very funny."

Will grouched. "At least them boys back then had coffee."

"We will, too," Slocum said. "Eventually."

Will got his rifle, muttering, "Promises, promises . . ."

There was movement across the way. Slocum and Will stiffened as a horse's ears, then head, came into sight.

Will raised his rifle.

"Wait!" hissed Slocum. "Give 'em time."

"You are one son of a bitch for givin' people time!" Will whispered. But he lowered his Henry just the same.

The horse proceeded to exit the cover of boulders, led by a man Slocum didn't recognize. Then another came out, then another, and finally, Bronc Dugan himself. All four men mounted up.

"Now?" Will asked.

"Wait."

The riders began to move down the canyon and toward them. "Goddamn it, Slocum!"

Dugan's men were within fifteen feet.

"Now!" Slocum cried, and pulled off two quick shots. Will did the same, but only three men fell. Dugan lashed his horse, fleeing past them down the canyon. Slocum got off three more shots, but Dugan was moving too fast and zigzagging too unpredictably.

"Damn it!" Slocum shouted, and leapt up on Apache. "Collect the bodies! I'll get Dugan!" He thundered out into the open and began the chase.

He knew he had to be careful. There was no rising trail of dust for him to follow, only muddy tracks in the patches of gravel between the scrub. And Dugan could cut out of sight at any moment and ambush him from behind the rocks or brush.

Back up the canyon, Will watched Slocum's silhouette vanish into the distance, then slowly walked across the way. He'd put his rifle away but brought out his handgun. He was taking no chances.

Once he had established that the men were dead for certain sure, he rounded up their horses. Or what was left of them. Somebody—probably him, although he'd never admit as much to Slocum—had shot one of their mounts, and now it lay groaning on the ground.

He knelt to it, rubbed its neck, then stood again. The wound was deep in the gut, and there was nothing to be done. Except . . .

"Sorry, ol' boy," he said softly, then shot the horse behind his eye. It was dead.

He slipped off the horse's bridle, because he figured that nothing should have to meet its maker with a chunk of iron in its mouth and leather straps round its head. It was a nice bridle, but he chucked it aside, then led the other horses back to where the outlaws' bodies lay.

Two horses and three bodies. It was a dilemma. He scratched at his chin for a moment before, in a sudden flash of brilliance, he decided what to do.

Slocum was at least a mile down the canyon before he reined Apache down to a walk. The horse was still game, but Slocum let him take a breather, just the same.

Dugan's tracks still showed that he was going flat out, and Slocum knew Dugan's mount couldn't stand up to this self-imposed pace for much longer. Maybe Dugan didn't care. He probably didn't. Any man who'd cut and run on his own gang members wouldn't give a good damn about his horse. He hadn't even glanced backward to see if any of them were still alive, Slocum realized.

Same old Bronc Dugan, the son of a bitch.

Slocum had run across Dugan a couple years back. Dugan was hot to have Slocum join forces with him— together, they'd clean out every bank west of the Mississippi, he said. And Slocum had said no, in no uncertain terms. He was trying to clean up his reputation, not sully it any further. Apparently, Dugan took it to heart. He had tried to kill Slocum the first chance he got.

Slocum was winged in the shoulder and shot in the back, and if it hadn't been for one Miss Caroline Corbus, he might have died. He slipped off his hat momentarily and said a kind word for Caroline. He hoped it would do some good. He didn't know how he was sitting with the Lord these days.

Ahead, Dugan's prints got closer together. He had slowed down his horse, finally, and he was moving at a walk. Slocum kept a sharper eye on the trail now. If Dugan had slowed up, it wasn't because he was easing his horse. But it might mean he was looking for a place to squirrel himself back in the rocks—and set his sights on Slocum. Or worse, Apache.

That sent a tingle up Slocum's spine. It's be just like Dugan to shoot the horse out from under him and shoot him while he scrambled for cover.

Of course, Dugan had no way of knowing that it was Slocum dogging his trail, let alone Will. He hadn't been riding an Appy back then—he'd been between spotted mounts and was, in fact, en route to Palouse country to pick up a new horse. Well, Dugan had sure thrown a wrench into his plans. He was six months late picking up that horse. Although all that time with Caroline Corbus had been a welcome vacation, even if he was sick as a dog for the better part of it. Her smile could have made the dead rise.

Well, it had sure made something rise anyway, in his case.

He pulled up Apache and twisted in the saddle, looking for any sign of Will. And there was none. All the man had to do was tie three corpses over their horses and follow him, for God's sake!

Sighing, he turned back around and urged Apache forward once more. He hadn't gone fifteen feet before the tracks suddenly veered off to the right, and he figured it was no coincidence that he was riding toward an area rich, once again, with boulders that had fallen from the slopes above. He veered in the opposite direction, figuring to catch Dugan at his own game.

He was nearly to the edge of the jagged line of boulders when a shot rang out. He heard it sing off a rock as he leapt off Apache and ran toward the sheltering stone. Just in time, too—another shot sang out, and splintered the rock behind which Slocum had taken cover.

Quickly, he shuffled down the narrow pass between

the fallen rock and the base of the cliff, pushing Apache's spotted backside in front of him. The farther he could work his position out of the direct line of Dugan's fire, the better. At least, until he could figure out exactly where the hell Dugan was.

Across the canyon floor—about forty feet across from one fallen line of rock to the other—and up a few yards, Dugan was increasingly frustrated with this interloper, this Nosey Parker, this moron who had not only killed his men, but then proceeded to *chase* him. Through Mexico, no less! He had no call to be chasing anybody south of the border, no call at all.

Actually, Dugan wasn't much bothered about losing his men. Men could be found anywhere, men that wanted to follow him. He wished he'd thought to grab the reins of one of their horses, though. He could always use a spare, and especially now. He was riding a bay mare, and she was about used up.

Well, once he put paid to this idiot across the way, he'd grab his Appy. Just who the hell did that fool think he was, anyhow? Didn't he know you didn't mess with Bronc Dugan without paying the consequences?

Dugan chanced another glance up over the ragged row of rough, craggy boulders piled in front of him. Still no sign of what he still assumed was a marshal, or that wild-colored horse of his. He'd caught one fleeting glimpse of the big man when he was jumping off his horse and heading for the rocks, and another—just the top of his hat, really—when he was farther down the way. But that was it.

He ground his teeth.

Just when he figured to have it made, just when his future looked clear and ripe, some jackass like this had to stick his nose into it. *It just figures, don't it?* he asked himself mutely. *Just when things was goin' halfway decent!*

Across the way, Slocum was hunkered down behind some boulders, reloading his handguns and rifle. At least last night's downpour had come from the west, so the canyon wall behind him had kept his position as dry as a bedroll—well, as dry as his bedroll usually was. It was still soaking from the storm, as were the clothes on his back.

He took a moment to peep over the rocks, but saw nothing but more rocks. No sign of Dugan, no sign of his horse. No sign of frigging anything!

For a moment, Slocum wondered why these bad boys didn't just step out into the open and say, "Go ahead and shoot. I'm over here!"

But they never did. They never learned. They never figured out that if you broke the law, somebody was going to chase you, and if you broke it bad enough, someone was going to kill you with a rope or a bullet, whichever came first. For such a bunch of yahoos as smart as they all, without exception, thought they were, they never figured any of it out.

He glanced behind him, up the canyon. Will was certainly taking his sweet time. How long did it take a fella to toss three bodies over their horses and follow him down here? But then he began to wonder if Will was planning on showing up. Ever. After all, he could get his money for those three back at the cave and never have to mess with Bronc Dugan. The Will Hutchins he used to know never would have done a thing like that, but then he hadn't known that Will Hutchins for a long time. Maybe things had changed.

He gave his head a quick shake, shaking the sense

back into it. Men didn't change that much. Will was coming, he was sure of it. He was just taking his sweet time about it, that was all.

Slocum hoped.

7

Back at Dugan's cave, Will was just finishing up. He'd had a lot to do. First, there was the loading of two bodies, one to a horse. And then there was the third body, with no horse left to haul it.

He'd copied something he'd seen Mexican bounty hunters do, although he had to admit it turned his stomach. He'd decapitated the third man, drained all the blood he could from the head, then bound it inside somebody's rainproof duster, after also pouring in all the booze he'd found on the site. He figured that the head was going to be pretty well pickled by the time it got back to whoever it was going to.

Having tied the packaged head to the saddle horn of one of the gang's stolen mounts, he at last mounted Duster, picked up the rope that was attached to the bridles of the two surviving horses, and set off down the canyon at a jog.

He just hoped Slocum would have the presence of mind to throw him a holler if Dugan had dug in somewhere and they were faced off. He wouldn't want to go to his maker when the last act he'd committed on this earth had been the grisly one of sawing off a man's head, even if the man had been an outlaw. And even if he'd already been dead at the time.

Dugan had fired first, and now Slocum had a place to aim at. When he had a chance to stick his head up over the rocks, that was. Shots rang out, sometimes staccato, sometimes legato. Slocum paused to reload once more, and stuck his head up over the rocks. No sign. He waited. Dugan had already winged him once, and he was bleeding from a graze over his right temple. He hoped Dugan was bleeding, too. A whole lot more than he was.

And if he wasn't bleeding already, Slocum planned to get him started.

There was still no sign of Will. Slocum began to hope that he'd heard the gun battle and had taken to the rocks.

The top of Dugan's head suddenly poked up into view, and Slocum fired automatically. Once, then twice. The hat didn't move, but he could see blood oozing from one of the holes in it. He hoped the bastard was dead, but he wasn't going to take any chances.

He waited. The hat didn't move, although the blood had stopped coursing from it. Dugan's horse had slowly wandered down behind the rocks, stopping near the hat as if it were waiting for something, when Will came into sight. He was leading two horses. Only two?

Slocum sent another bullet straight up into the air, a warning shot. Will dismounted and led his horses over to the side of the canyon—Slocum's side, since Slocum had owned the presence of mind to wave his rifle barrel, purposefully disclosing his position.

There were still no signs of life from across the canyon. Slocum took a tentative step out.

Still no signs of life.

He leaned his rifle up against the rocks, but drew his handgun. He wasn't going across there without some backup, no matter how superstitious it sounded.

But when he arrived, he found he hadn't needed to worry. Dugan was still alive, all right, but he was out cold. That bullet that had made him get blood all over his (probably stolen) hat had only grazed his head—but knocked him out six ways from Sunday.

Slocum hollered out to Will, letting him know everything was under control, then bound and gagged the unconscious Dugan. Better safe than sorry, he figured. Then he boosted Dugan's limp form up over his saddle and roped him down, lest he slip off to one side or the other.

About the time he finished, Will came walking up, leading the horses. He had gathered up Apache on his way.

"He dead?" Will asked, nodding toward Dugan.

"Only wishes he was," replied Slocum as he pushed past Will and led the horse out into the canyon proper. "He's out cold."

Will shook his head. "Shame."

Slocum glanced over at the horses Will had brought down. "What happened to the third corpse?" There was a horse missing, too.

"I sort of shot his horse," Will replied sheepishly.

"Body back up there?"

"Nope." Will poked a thumb at the parcel hanging from his saddle horn. "In there."

Slocum stood there a second, letting it sink in. "You didn't. Did you?"

"I did it with my little axe, Papa Washington," Will said with a straight face. "Well, more like my big ol' Bowie knife. Then pickled it with all the booze they had on 'em. Quite a bit, actually, even with me drinkin' it as I went. Gotta keep from throwin' up, y'know."

Slocum could well imagine, but didn't say anything. The less Will talked about puking, the less the chance that Slocum would give in to the urge, too.

He swung his leg up over Apache. He'd already put Dugan's rope around his horse's neck, and now he dallied it to Apache's saddle horn. "Let's get goin'."

Will mounted, too. "Where?"

"North." Slocum didn't give a damn about the destination so long as it was somewhere above the border. And he wanted to get there fast. Eventually, those bodies were going to start stinking to high heaven. Dugan wasn't going to stay unconscious forever, either.

Will shrugged. "Onward, then," he said, and started back up the canyon, leading the two body-toting mounts. "C'mon, boys," he said to the horses. "Your daddies miss you."

Slocum snorted.

"Well, they do," said Will, raising his voice a bit.

Slocum smiled. "Yeah," he admitted, "reckon they do. Can we move it up into a jog?"

"Anything you want, anything you want," Will said, and urged Duster into a trot while he clucked to the horses behind him.

Slocum was actually happy, and he relaxed into a smile. They'd caught their quarry and were headed back home. Pretty soon, he and Will would be divvying up twenty grand. A man could buy a lot of women, champagne, and good cigars with ten grand.

He certainly could.

SLOCUM AND THE SONORAN FUGITIVE 51

* * *

They camped that night just a few miles south of the border. Slocum would have liked to push on through the dark, but Will wasn't having it.

"I'm tired," he'd said after they'd been arguing more than twenty minutes, "and I ain't ridin' no farther."

And then he'd climbed down off his horse and started gathering wood.

Slocum had given up. Maybe if he gave on this, Will'd give on something more important. He could only hope, couldn't he?

If anybody was thrilled to be stopping, it was Dugan. He'd woken late that afternoon, and since his mouth was gagged, he'd been moaning for the last hour and a half. Slocum knew his head hurt without him jawing about it endlessly. He figured the Arizona Territory would take care of that little headache for him, and in short order.

If anybody had ever deserved it, it was Dugan. In Slocum's opinion, that was. Will had offered to do it already, three times just this afternoon. Slocum supposed it didn't really matter. The man was going to die anyway. But it was the principle of the thing, if such things as principles could be applied to a man who was wanted "Dead or Alive." Slocum wasn't sure, but he was leaning toward the opinion that they didn't.

He dismounted Apache and tied him to a bush before he went back and began untying the ropes that bound Dugan to his saddle. He bet that Dugan's belly was sorer than hell. He'd ridden a long way in that ungainly position. Undignified, too, Slocum thought with a smile as he unbound the last foot, growled, "C'mon back down, Dugan," and pulled his prisoner to the ground by his belt.

Dugan landed clumsily and nearly fell. But Slocum

caught him and settled him firmly on his feet. It wasn't that he was being kindly. There were too many tricky things a man on the ground could do to you—knock your feet out from under you, head-butt you, and on and on—for him to take the chance.

Dugan was making sounds through his gag, sounds like he wanted Slocum to remove it, for instance. But Slocum didn't, not yet. First, he dragged Dugan over to a clear space on the ground, where Will had already dumped his first load of branches and scrub. Slocum sat Dugan on the ground, checked his ankle rope and the ropes around his wrists, and only then did he remove the gag.

"About fuckin' time!" Dugan shouted. And then he took a closer look at Slocum. "You ain't no marshal! I know you, from a long time back." His face worked as he tried to figure it out.

"I'll save you the trouble," Slocum said. "I'm John Slocum. You tried to recruit me for your gang once. And when I wasn't interested, you tried to murder me. Almost made good on it, if'n that makes you feel any better."

Dugan grunted. After a moment, he said, "So why you after me now?"

"Reward," Slocum said simply. He turned his back and walked over to the horses. "You're worth a good bit of money." He came up with enough rope to hobble all the horses, and set to work on it.

Behind him, Dugan said, "Enough to come all the way down to Mexico. You're one unforgivin' bastard."

"No. I just like working legal for a livin'."

Will dropped another load of kindling and wood into the open space, announcing his presence. Slocum looked up and said, "Looks like enough to keep us goin' for a while."

Will was staring at Dugan, who glared at him and said, "And what'd I do to you? Steal your penny candy? Your girl? Your horse?"

Will didn't answer him. He just started laying the fire.

"Well, will somebody untie my hands?" Dugan practically shouted. "I gotta piss."

Slocum finished tying the last hobble and started stripping off Apache's tack. "So do it. Your hands're tied in front, y'know." How stupid did Dugan think they were?

"Oh," Dugan said. "So they are, so they are . . ."

"Don't help him, Will," Slocum cautioned. He pulled off Apache's saddle and slid it to the ground.

"Wasn't gonna," Will grumped. "Let the son of a bitch figure it out for himself."

Well, Slocum had meant *Don't let him near your sidearm, 'cause he'll shoot you—or your knife, lest he gut you like a fish,* but he didn't say anything more. He figured Will was smart enough to know that already.

When he finished with Apache, he carried the saddle over to the infant fire and laid out his bedroll opposite Dugan. Dugan hadn't made it all the way up to his feet, his ankles being bound. But he'd made it to his knees and was still pissing. Which got Will started, too—his fourth leak break this afternoon—but at least he walked out of camp a ways before he let loose.

Slocum walked back and pulled the two outlaws' bodies down, then pulled the saddles and bridles from their horses, as well, before he opened Apache's water bag and gave all the horses, Dugan's included, a good long drink. When he'd worked his way down the line to Will's Duster, Will had already taken off his tack.

"Thanks for gettin' him hobbled, Slocum," he said.

"No problem." Slocum offered more water to Duster, who took it greedily. "What's for supper?"

"You'll take what you can get," Will replied with a trace of a smile. He lifted his tack and headed for the infant fire.

Chuckling, Slocum shook his head.

8

Dugan slept well that night, but not so Slocum and Will. They took shifts standing guard—two hours on, two hours off. When Slocum woke him the next morning, Will was pretty damn cantankerous.

"Don't know why you just didn't shoot him all the way dead," Will grumped. "I coulda got a whole night's sleep, insteada up, down, up, down . . ."

"Cup a' coffee make you feel any better?" Slocum held out a mug filled with fresh brew. He'd just poured it.

Will took his cup and had a sip. "Good," he said, nodding despite a partial scowl still left on his face. "You make breakfast, too?"

Slocum nodded. "Bacon and eggs. If you're up to it."

"Where'd you find a chicken out here?" Will asked, surprised.

"Didn't," Slocum replied. He got Will a couple of eggs, over easy, and a few slices of bacon, then handed him the plate. "Found 'em in Dugan's saddlebags. Seems they stole more'n the horses."

Around a mouthful of bacon, Will said, "So mebbe he ain't all bad." He smiled a little.

"Don't go gettin' all hearts and flowers on me, Will," Slocum said. He filled another plate, found a fork, then rose and walked around the fire. He kicked the bottom of Dugan's boot. "Wake up, if you wanna have any breakfast."

Dugan opened his eyes, then sat up and reached for the plate Slocum held out.

Although Slocum was ready for any trick he might pull, Dugan simply took the plate and asked, "That coffee I smell?"

Slocum fetched him a cup of coffee while Will wandered off to take a leak. He'd best have that taken care of, and soon, Slocum thought. He'd been up several times during the night, too, while Slocum was on watch.

When Will came back and got settled with his plate once more, Slocum finally scraped his breakfast out of the skillet and onto a plate and dug in. He was a pretty decent campfire cook, if he said so himself. When they were all finished, Will cleaned the plates and Dugan lolled, his back against a rock, while Slocum began saddling the horses.

"You feed 'em already?" Will asked.

"And watered." Slocum nodded toward the bodies on the ground. "Those two are startin' to smell already. We can't take 'em back up to Monkey Springs. Gotta take 'em to some place bigger."

"Some place with a bigger bank, you mean." Will grinned.

Slocum returned the expression. "Yeah, that too." He snugged Apache's girth. "Some place with a halfway sober sheriff is more important. You know that nobody's gonna just hand over twenty grand in cash. They're gonna give us vouchers, period."

Will looked up. "Tombstone."

It was a good idea. It was only a day farther than Monkey Springs, and Slocum knew the sheriff. Make that the marshal. Tombstone was a county seat.

"Good thinking," Slocum said aloud. "I know the Earp boys. They'll cut us a fair deal. Now, Behan's a pain in the butt, but we won't be havin' to deal with him."

Will asked, "Who's Behan?"

"Town sheriff." Slocum had moved on to the stolen horses by this time. He slung the first dead body up across a saddle and proceeded to rope it into place.

"You really oughta take me up to Monkey Springs, boys," piped up Dugan. "After all, they'll be needin' their horses, won't they?"

"Shut up, Dugan," both Will and Slocum said at the same time.

By noon, they had crossed over into the U.S. and were navigating their way through the Santa Rita Mountains. This was easier than it sounded, because Slocum knew the Santa Ritas like the back of his hand.

They had traveled through one pass—with Dugan tied, as yesterday, across his saddle—and were climbing up to take the second, when Will had to whoa up and wander off to take another leak. It was getting ridiculous, if you asked Slocum. Good thing that Will had settled down in Prescott, where they had lots of outhouses. Slocum would be glad to send him on his way back home—something he'd be able to do once they turned in Dugan and the bodies and picked up their vouchers.

Which left him wondering—just what the hell would he do with ten thousand dollars? He could only spend so much on women, cards, and wine before it got old. What would he do then? In truth, he'd never considered that they might actually get the whole of the Dugan gang and actually get paid for them. Things like that had a way of not working out for him. But they would make Tombstone by dark, and then it would become a reality.

He had half a mind to just cut Dugan's ropes, let him run, and turn in the other three for half the money. But the thought, like most bad ideas, only came and went.

"Thanks," Will said. He had returned and was climbing back on his mount.

Dugan growled something or other through his gag and slid a nasty look toward Slocum, who chose to ignore it.

He said, "No thanks needed. I believe we'll make Tombstone by dark."

They moved out, Slocum leading Dugan's horse, Will leading the other two uphill, through the rocky gorge that would let them pass between the jagged peaks of two mountains, then lead them down toward the rolling flatland of Tombstone.

"Brought you a present, fellas," Slocum said as he dragged Dugan through the door of the law office, then plopped him down in a chair.

"Well, I'll be damned!" said one of the lawmen, not the tallest but the youngest in the room. "If it ain't John Slocum come to call! Virgil, c'mon out here and see what the wind blew in!"

Virgil stepped out of the back room about the same time that Will followed Slocum through the front door. Virgil was tall and lean and fair, like his younger brother, and he wore the U.S. marshal's badge. He stuck out his hand and took Slocum's eagerly. "Well, I'll be codswalloped! Good to see you, Slocum." He nodded toward the bench against the wall. "Who's your hogtied friend?"

Slocum said, "Bronc Dugan, who I understand you're lookin' for. Got three of his buddies—well, two whole and a part of another—outside, too."

"Dugan!" Virgil hissed, his eyes narrowing as he glared at the figure. "No shit! Where in the hell'd you catch up to him?"

"Down 'round the border country," Will injected, then introduced himself. "Will Hutchins, that's me. Used to be in your line of work."

"Till his bladder caught up with him," Slocum said softly, but nobody was paying attention. He was fine with that because he was really hoping to see Wyatt. There were a whole passel of Earps—five brothers, or was it six?—who had all come west together. They'd been up in Kansas for a while, but recently most of them had moved farther west and south, to the promising little mining town of Tombstone, Arizona Territory, formerly known as Goose Flats.

Tombstone might have started as nothing, but ever since Ed Sheifflin had found silver, it was a hell's-a-poppin' town. Slocum wondered, for the first time, if Tombstone might actually be able to pay cash for the owlhoots he'd just brought in.

Virgil and Will were still carrying on, but he broke in. "Virgil, I don't suppose Wyatt's in town, is he?"

Virgil shook his head. "Nope. Me and Morgan's in charge of the store for the time bein'." He nodded toward his brother. "Wyatt, he had to run up to Tucson for a few days. Gonna meet up with Warren whilst he's there."

Slocum had never heard of Warren, but it was safe to guess that he was another brother.

"Be back come Friday, though," Morgan added.

"Can we get Dugan inside a cell?" Will asked.

Virgil had the keys dangling in his hand. "Sure thing, sure thing," he said. "Morgan, you wanna take care'a them dead boys outside?"

Morgan Earp said, "You got it," and walked to the door. Opening it, he stretched his arm out to point at the parcel hanging from one of the saddle horns. To Will, he asked, "That thing all you brought of number three?"

"Yup."

"Believe I'll put 'em down to the stable, Virge," Morgan said, and went on outside.

"Those are stolen horses. The ones they're on, I mean, and the bay that transported Dugan. They grabbed 'em in Monkey Springs," Slocum said.

"There were four all together," Will added. Slocum figured he had to pee again, because he was hopping from foot to foot. "One of 'em caught a bullet durin' the battle. I'll pay for it, if'n it's a big loss to the owner."

Virgil started to nod his agreement, but Slocum said, "Don't worry about it, Will. I'll take care of it. I can drop over to Monkey Springs in a couple days, take 'em back myself, and pay for the dead one." He paused. "Hell, you got a horse trader in town?"

Virgil smiled. "Be surprised if we didn't have a few."

Slocum nodded. "Believe I'll look one up in the morning. Fella livin' clear out in Monkey Springs oughta be happier with a good replacement than the cash value, wouldn't you figure?"

"Indeed I would," said Virgil. "You boys'll be wantin' your money, I reckon?"

Will brightened. "You reckon rightly."

* * *

After the Earps got the identities of the dead men straight, Virgil wrote out two vouchers for ten thousand dollars each and handed one to Will and one to Slocum. "That'll do 'er, boys," he said, fingering his mustache.

"No, it won't," said Slocum, and pulled his guns from their holsters. "I'm stayin' overnight."

Morgan went over to a large chest that stood against the far wall and stuck a key in the lock. Virgil handed him the guns, and Morgan said, "You know yours on sight?"

Virgil chuckled softly, but Slocum, sober as a judge, said, "Yeah, I do."

Morgan asked Will the same question and got the same response. After he locked the chest again, he said, "Virgil, you quit snickerin'. You know we gotta ask."

Virgil let out a full-throated laugh before he said, "It just seems real funny, you askin' John Slocum and a former U.S. marshal that question, that's all. Sorry, Morgan." And then he broke out in laughter again.

With a muttered "Aw, jeez," Morgan retired to the back room.

"You might wanna feed him some supper," Slocum said, poking a thumb toward the back room where the cells were. "We didn't stop on the way into town."

"Gotcha," replied Virgil.

Will looked like he had to get out of there in a hurry, or embarrass them all. Slocum took pity on him. "See you tomorrow!" he said to Virgil, then hollered, "Thanks, Morgan!" toward the door.

He and Will slipped outside. Will said, "Thank God!," ducked into an alley, and began pissing his brains out. This was accompanied by long, lingering sighs.

A chuckle underscoring his words, Slocum said, "You pissin' or gettin' a blow job, Will?"

Still peeing, Will said, "Real funny, Slocum. You oughta go on the stage."

"And there's one leavin' at noon," laughed Slocum. "I know, I know . . ."

9

Slocum was feeling pretty full of himself. He and Will had caught their prey, turned them in, and they had their vouchers. Slocum had already decided that in the morning, he was going to open a bank account with his and get as much cash as he could. That way, he'd always have money in Tombstone. Or he supposed he could have it transferred someplace else, if the spirit so moved him at a later date. But he wasn't going to take one step out of town with that ten-thousand-dollar voucher in his pocket!

He took Will up to the Oriental—they had gambling and drinking and entertainment, along with rooms—and they sat at a corner table, ordering beer. Well, Will ordered beer. Slocum ordered a beer, to be followed by an iced bucket of champagne. He also ordered himself a good cigar.

That took care of a good chunk of it.

While they sipped their beer, Slocum took a long look around the room, which was shaped like an L. Around the corner, he could see somebody sitting where

Wyatt usually did while he was in town, dealing faro.
Slocum didn't much care for faro. The house had too
much going for it, if you asked him. There were several
poker games in progress around the room, too, and he
began to check out the players, mentally tagging the
professional cardsharps for later reference.

He didn't see Doc Holliday, though, and this left him
a bit perplexed. Well, maybe Doc was someplace up the
street, plying his trade. Doc was the kind of man who
could have just as easily been Slocum's enemy, had they
not been introduced by Wyatt. He had come to appreciate Doc's wry sense of humor as well as his dogged
devotion to Wyatt. From afar, he had already admired
his devil-may-care accuracy with firearms.

Somebody somewhere was singing a lively song—
"Three Cheers for Billy," he thought it was, although it
was hard to make it out through the crowd noise. The
female voice got him thinking about womanly companionship, and he changed the focus of his scan.

There were plenty of girls prowling the tables and the
bar for customers. White, Chinese, Mex, tame Indian—
it looked like he could have his pick. He had just about
made his choice and was going to signal a little blond
girl standing by the bar, when from behind him, a female voice said, "Well, hello there, Slocum."

He turned around, and a grin suddenly spread over
his face, unbidden. He cried, "Mandy!" and reached
back for her, dragging her into his lap. He was hard already.

She knew it the second she sat down. Hugging
Slocum's neck, she gave him a big wet kiss on his stub-
bly cheek and said, "What the hell are you doin' in
Tombstone, handsome?"

"Dropped by to see Wyatt," he said. He didn't dare

tell her the whole truth, especially not down here where anybody could overhear.

"You're outta luck," she said. "He's—"

"Not here," Slocum interrupted. "We heard already. Mandy, meet my trail companion, Will Hutchins. Will, this is Mandy Adams."

Will tipped his hat and said, "Ma'am. Slocum, when you think they're gonna deliver that French stuff a' yours?" He looked eagerly toward the bar. He'd told Slocum earlier that he'd never had champagne before, and it seemed he was looking forward to giving it a try.

Just then, a bartender approached bearing an ornate silver bucket, which was placed on Slocum and Will's table. There was a bottle in it, surrounded by chopped ice. Now, where the hell did they come by ice in a town like Tombstone? Slocum was too eager to settle down to drinking to ask. He motioned to the barkeep to go ahead and open it, which the man did with great fanfare, and a spurt of the bubbly wine that almost hit the ceiling.

"Whoa!" Will laughed.

Slocum and Mandy laughed along with him, as did the old man by the bar who'd caught part of the champagne spurt in his open mouth.

"Three glasses?" the barkeep asked.

Slocum nodded, and soon he, Will, and Mandy were all holding champagne glasses. "Here's to Tombstone," Slocum said by way of a toast, and they all tipped their glasses back.

Will drained his in one gulp, then grinned. "Say, this is pretty good stuff!"

"It tickles!" giggled Mandy, and took another sip.

Slocum drank his slowly, savoring the sweet, crisp taste, although he said, "Coulda chilled a mite longer."

He and Will sat in the Oriental Saloon for another

hour, sipping champagne—Slocum had to order a second bottle—and listening to Mandy chatter away about old times. Slocum had first known her in East Texas, and the last place he'd seen her was over in Santa Fe. She was a petite blonde, full-breasted and tiny-waisted, and he was amazed that she still looked so young and fresh. Hers wasn't an easy trade to ply. He knew the girls often had trouble with their customers, especially in bawdy mining towns like this.

He sure wasn't planning on giving her any problems, though. He grinned. He was still hanging on to her for dear life.

"Hit me again, buddy," Will slurred, and held out his glass. Slocum figured Will had pissed away a good bottle of that champagne, since he'd already gone to the outhouse three times since their arrival.

But he lifted the bottle and poured anyway. Will deserved this. So did he. Hell, it wasn't every day that you brought in twenty grand's worth of outlaws!

And it wasn't every day that he had a lapful of Mandy Adams, either.

He poured out the last of the bottle into his and Mandy's glasses and put it back in the ice bucket upside down. He toasted, "Here's to wine, woman, song, and sleepin' inside on a real bed."

Will said, "I'll second that!" and slurped his drink back.

Mandy purred, "I like the sound of that bed part. You got a private room, honey?"

"Not yet, but I'm about to," Slocum said. "You wanna excuse me for a second, Mandy?"

"Don't be long, Slocum," she teased, fluttering long lashes over blue eyes.

* * *

Slocum got himself and Will each a room—the last two left, as luck would have it—and they all went upstairs. After he gently placed Will on his hotel bed and wished him good night, he and Mandy found his room.

"You figure you still got that rock in your pants?" Mandy whispered infectiously as he unlocked the door. "You know, the one I sat on downstairs?"

Slocum ushered her in, then locked the door behind them. Grinning, he said, "I reckon it's plaguin' me again already, honey girl," and stripped off his shirt.

She joined him in the bed in slap time, both of them naked as jaybirds. How could she have stayed so youthful? Time had marred him more times than he could count with its implements of death—scars from countless Indian skirmishes, knife fights, and gun battles had added themselves to the patchwork of welted tissue that covered him—but she looked very much like that young girl from East Texas he'd first met in the Dallas Queen Saloon.

Funny, that he'd remembered that all these years later.

She was dewy-skinned and fresh, with rosy color in her cheeks and lips. Her breasts were still high and full and round, and still tipped with that particular pink distinct to blondes with her pale coloration, like the inside of a seashell. The only difference that he could see were the long, pale scars that covered her abdomen. It took him a few moments to realize that they were stretch marks, and that she'd once carried a baby.

He put his thumb on one faint line and asked, "What happened to it?"

She looked embarrassed and turned away from him.

Softly, she said, "He died when he was only a week old. I never did figure out who his daddy was. I was in a mining camp when he started growin' in me, so it was probably a miner. Somebody back in New Mexico. Somebody who's probably moved on."

Slocum turned her back to face him. "I'm sorry, Mandy."

She smiled a little. "Thanks, Slocum. Y'know, after, the doc said I wouldn't be able to have any more. He was right. Nothin's took root in me since then." She smiled again, but he could tell it was forced. "Guess it was good for me, professionally."

He kissed her temple gently. "It's all right, baby girl," he whispered as he took her into his arms. She began to weep softly against his chest, and he repeated, "It's all right, it's all right," over and over.

After about a half hour, he felt her shift position, and she looked up at him, red-nosed, but dry-eyed. She whispered, "Thanks, Slocum. I know that babysittin' a bawling woman wasn't what you bargained for. It's just, well, nobody ever asked before. About Charlie. That's what I called him, you know."

"It's a good name," he said. "Strong."

Her brows arched. "Not strong enough, I guess." She smiled a little and reached back to grasp his member, which suddenly bloomed at her touch. She put on a fake Mexican accent. "Not strong like ze bool!" she said as, smiling, she gave him a little tug.

He stiffened some more. If she didn't get on with it pretty damned soon, he was going to explode in her hand. He opened his mouth to tell her, but he didn't have to. She was already climbing on top of him, straddling him.

Her body poised just above his, she stopped. "Slocum, you're a good man," she breathed just before she slowly slid down on his shaft, conjoining their bodies and enveloping him in her moist heat.

"Jesus, Mandy!" he grunted as she began to move, first grinding down, then rising so that just the head of his member was within her, swirling, then grinding down again.

"He's got nothing to do with this," she said with a giggle as she continued to move.

He couldn't take much more of this, but he wanted her to come, too. He reached for her breasts and took them both into his hands, kneading the nipples until they were hard as pebbles. She obviously liked this, because she bent forward to make it easier for him and whispered, "Yes, Slocum, yes!"

She kept moving on him, never giving him a moment to collect himself, kept moving inexorably up and down, back and forth. He had the presence of mind to bring one breast to his lips and latch hold of the nipple, suckling strongly on the tight bud.

He felt her kiss his brow just before she started making those low, throaty sounds that told him she was coming. They became more rapid, deeper, and then they both lost control. He began to buck his hips up into her as she stiffened, holding herself still so that he was in control. As if he had any at this stage!

And he came, exploding inside her so thunderously that for a second, he wondered if he was going to live through it.

But he did.

As always.

And he caught her when she collapsed down into his

arms and onto his chest, panting and sweating and sated. Not everything changed, he thought as he stroked her back. No, some things stayed exactly the same. And Mandy was one of them.

10

The next morning, Slocum woke early. Sunlight streamed through the eastern windows, making the room around him look crisp and clean. Mandy slept beside him, in the same position she'd gone to sleep in—curled against his side, her arm thrown casually across his chest. He gently moved her arm and slithered out of the bed. He had to take a leak and reached under the bed, feeling until he found the chamber pot.

Afterward, he was about to climb back in next to her when somebody's knuckles rapped at the door. He made a face and thought, *If that's Will, I'm gonna kill him.*

But he pulled on his britches, tossed a sheet over Mandy, and went to the door. He opened it to find a familiar face, but it wasn't Will's.

"Wyatt!" he exclaimed, and stuck out his hand, shaking Wyatt's enthusiastically. "You old dog! Glad to see you. I'd invite you in, but—"

Wyatt didn't wait for him to finish the sentence. He just barged into the room and very seriously said,

"Slocum, old buddy, I'm glad to see you, too, but I need your help."

Slocum blinked. "You need my help?" He was puzzled, to say the least. Why would this famous lawman need his help?

"Bronc Dugan broke out last night."

At first, Slocum didn't believe him. He barked out a laugh that was cut short by Wyatt's dead serious expression.

Slocum said, "You're not jokin', are you?"

"He somehow thumped Morgan and let himself out, then walked down to the livery, stole a horse, and left. Went south, we think."

"How's Morgan?"

"Gonna be fine. He was lucky that it was the middle of the night. We figure Dugan wanted to keep things quiet."

Slocum shook his head. "Well, shit. So what you want me for?" he asked, although he thought he knew.

Wyatt didn't look the least bit apologetic. He said, "Need you to help me track him down, Slocum. You and your partner."

From the bed, Mandy moaned a little in her sleep, and Wyatt had the decency to color a little. "Sorry, Slocum. Didn't realize you had company."

Slocum waved a hand and said, "S'all right. This is important."

"Glad to hear you say that. How soon can you leave?"

Across the room, Mandy sat up, the sheet around her. She rubbed at her eyes, then smiled and said, "Mornin' Slocum, Wyatt. To what do we owe this honor? And why're you back so soon?"

"Mornin', Mandy." Wyatt tipped his hat and said,

"Serendipity, I 'magine. And I'm here to talk your boy-friend into lendin' the legalities a helpin' hand."

She snugged the sheet around her chin and lay back down. "Just don't go keepin' him too long."

"Do my best not to," Wyatt replied with another tip of his hat, along with a full-fledged grin.

"Got to wake up my partner and grab some break-fast," Slocum said, fingering his chin. "Half an hour all right?"

"Yeah," said Wyatt. He turned and put his hand on the knob, before he looked back. "Oh, by the way, Slocum, that horse Dugan stole?"

"Yeah?"

"He was yours."

Slocum found himself in the grip of a surge of adrenaline. Through clenched teeth, he said, "Fifteen minutes."

Will was sick, and he wasn't going. He was so sick, in fact, that he actually agreed to go see Doc Goodnight.

"What's wrong, aside from you pissin' every five minutes?" Slocum had asked him. Rather callously, too, he thought later, for somebody who'd been pushing him six ways from Sunday to go to a damn doctor.

"Got an ache in my belly," he'd moaned, and Slocum didn't push him any further.

He'd just let Will know where he was going, and re-minded him to drop by the bank as soon as he could to get that voucher off his hands. "You just hang around the place and wait for me," Slocum had said. "Won't be more'n a few days, I don't imagine."

Slocum himself had made a hurried dash to the bank, where he opened an account, relieved himself of his voucher, and pulled out two hundred in cash before he made haste for the livery. There, he bought a nice sorrel gelding—not an Appy, but nice, nonetheless—with three white socks and a star. Sound, too. He figured he wouldn't own him long, so he decided to just call him Red.

When he finally ended up at the jail, Wyatt was waiting for him impatiently. "Fifteen minutes, on the nose," Wyatt said, but he said it as if he wished Slocum had done it quicker.

Wyatt mounted up, and Slocum asked, "Where's Virgil?"

"Inside." Wyatt turned his horse away from the rail before he said, "Oh. You'll be wantin' these." He dug inside his coat, pulled out Slocum's handguns, and handed them over. "Where's your pal?"

Slocum shoved the Colts into their holsters. "Sick. Ain't comin'." He started out of town, right along next to Wyatt. "Gonna go see Doc Goodnight."

Wyatt nodded. "Virgil's got county business to attend to."

"Oh." Slocum didn't know why the "county business" couldn't wait for a few days. He would have appreciated Virgil's company, and he told Wyatt as much.

"We have to take the best we can get," Wyatt said. "I figure you're the best that I could get. And vice versa, I hope."

Slocum had no argument with that, although he was wishing that he'd taken Will's advice and just put a slug into Dugan's brain when he had a chance. It sure would have saved him a load of work and worry. Would have saved his horse, too. He didn't say it to Wyatt—after all, he'd been willing to go along before he'd heard that the son of a bitch had stolen his horse—but he was more anxious to get Apache back than to find Dugan. He hoped Dugan wouldn't run the Appy too long or too hard.

He hoped Dugan wouldn't kill him.

With this fervent wish gnawing at him, he and Wyatt rode south, out of Tombstone.

They started out at a lope and held it for a while, and when they slowed to a walk to let the horses have a breather, Slocum lit a quirley. Wyatt lit a slim black cigar.

"Hope he bypassed Bisbee," Slocum said between drags. "I've got a decent eye for his tracks, and we'll surely lose 'em if he goes through a town."

"Mayhap that's why he'll do it," Wyatt said.

"Don't be so hopeful."

"Can't help it. It's my nature."

Slocum took another drag. Something had been bothering him. He said, "Where's Doc? Ain't he usually around?"

"Doc's down to Bisbee. If we have to track Dugan through there, mayhap he'll join up with us."

Slocum nodded. "I'd like that. Been a coon's age. He still got the lung thing?" He was referring to Doc's tuberculosis, the reason he had come west in the first place.

"'Bout the same. Last time you seen him was up in Kansas, wasn't it?"

Slocum grinned. "Last time I seen any of you. You're lookin' good, Wyatt."

Wyatt nodded, his mustache bobbing slightly. "Thank'e. Try to keep myself from getting killed."

"A wise move. Same here, 'cept people keep on shootin' me up."

"Well, I ain't had that trouble. So far, anyway. Knock wood."

"You always had the damnedest luck of any man I ever did meet, Wyatt," Slocum said with admiration. It was true, too.

"Like I said, knock wood."

* * *

Dugan, indeed, had gone through Bisbee. His tracks—distinctive because Apache toed in, just slightly, with his off hind hoof, and had been shod to correct it with a shoe print that Slocum could recognize—took them right into town before they were lost in the scuffled dust of a hundred others.

Wyatt rode straight to the hotel and inquired about Doc.

The clerk checked the ledger, saying, "Nope. Believe he checked out . . . Here it is." He swiveled the book around so that Wyatt and Slocum could see. "Checked out yesterday at four in the afternoon."

Wyatt asked, "Say where he was goin'?"

The clerk shook his head. "Thought it was kinda funny, since there weren't any stages that late. Course, he may'a rode into town. Still, it's a funny time to start horsebackin'. Closest town is up north, 'bout a day's ride."

"Tombstone," Wyatt said with a nod. "We just came from there."

"Must've missed him on the way south," Slocum said. Since they'd been following Dugan's tracks, and Dugan hadn't taken the conventional route south, it was entirely possible.

Wyatt nodded, and got them a room for the night. It was nearly dark outside.

Afterward, Slocum took the horses to the livery, while Wyatt took their saddlebags and portable gear upstairs.

Slocum checked out the livery horses while he was at the stable. He didn't find Apache, but he asked the boy on duty about him. "You see a bright sorrel Appaloosa in town today? Woulda been a medium-sized feller, kinda reddish hair, ridin' him."

"I just come on duty, mister," the boy said. "So I ain't seen nothin'. But Bob mighta."

He closed Red's stall, latching him in, the walked back to the office. "Hey, Bob!" he shouted, then repeated Slocum's question.

Bob, who remained hidden behind the office door, mumbled something Slocum couldn't make out, and then the boy came jogging back. "Said he seen a horse like that tied to the rail over by the Happy Rooster Saloon this mornin'," he told Slocum, slightly winded. He pointed up the street. "That way. But he's gone now. Bob says when he took his lunch, the horse was gone and he ain't seen him since."

Slocum nodded his thanks, and when he left the livery, he walked up the street anyway. A half block later, he crossed the street and walked into the Happy Rooster. It was a fair-sized saloon full of miners and the like. But no Dugan. Apache hadn't been on the rail, either.

He made his way over to the bar and asked the barkeep, "Were you on duty this mornin'?"

When the barkeep nodded yes, Slocum asked him if he remembered Dugan.

The barkeep's formerly smiling face suddenly crunched into a mask of wrinkles. "Bastard was in here, all right," he said. "You a friend of his?"

Slocum guessed that any friend of Dugan's was not welcome in this bar, so he told the truth. "Nope. He escaped from the Tombstone jail last night, stole a horse, and I'm trackin' 'em."

"Well, this mornin' he started a fight in here," the bartender began. "Sent two'a the regulars to the doc, and busted my good long mirror." He pointed to a lengthy vacant spot on the opposite wall. "Had that mirror shipped in all the way from St. Louis! Man's a troublemaker! Glad you told me his name, partner." He pulled up a sawed-off shotgun from behind the bar and brandished it. "That shitheel Dugan ain't never gonna get another chance to bust up my place!"

"I'll do my best to see he never gets another chance," Slocum said. He tipped his hat. "Thank you kindly. Oh. What time'd he leave?"

"Musta been around eleven or so. Does it matter?"

Slocum nodded. "Yeah, it does. Thanks again."

11

Slocum walked back up to the hotel to give Wyatt the news. He'd been concerned that Dugan was getting too far ahead of them. "How long can a man go without sleep before he has to stop, anyway?" he asked Wyatt after he'd told him Dugan's story.

"Good question," Wyatt said noncommittally.

Slocum wouldn't be put off with a shrug, though. "Reckon it varies from man to man?"

"Yeah. Let's go get us some dinner so we can get to bed early. Want to be up and at 'em by dawn. Okay by you?"

Slocum gave a quick nod. "Yeah, just dandy." He would rather have hit the trail again tonight, though. Time was passing, and Dugan was getting farther and farther away while they'd be sitting around someplace, eating a steak.

They walked down the stairs, and when they were almost outside, Wyatt stopped, his hand on the latch, and said, "You'd druther be out on the trail, wouldn't you?"

Slocum didn't hesitate. "Yup."

"Well, why the hell didn't you say somethin'?"

"You're the marshal, so you're in charge," Slocum said. It was simply a statement of fact.

Wyatt let out air in a long hiss. "Slocum, I left my badge back in Tombstone with Virgil, in case you didn't notice. I ain't no marshal for this trip. We're just a couple of private citizens out on a hunt."

Relief washed over Slocum. He said, "Well, why didn't you tell a feller?"

Wyatt shrugged his shoulders. "Didn't think I had to. Well, c'mon. Let's get us some dinner before we head out again."

Slocum was much happier with this plan. They exited the hotel, found a café, and ordered a steak each, plus some fixings. When it came to the table, they didn't waste any time talking or dawdling. They were business-like in eating, and paid their bill.

They were back on the trail by six.

It was growing dark already, but Slocum still kept his eye to the ground, watching for signs of Apache's peculiar hind hoofprint.

They had chosen the right road. About a quarter mile out of town, Slocum found sign, mixed in with the prints of twenty other horses. Apache had stepped in a clear spot, one of very few on the trail.

"Got him!" Slocum cried.

"'Bout damn time," Wyatt said, teasing.

"Now we just gotta catch him." Slocum looked up. The moon was up and full in a sky free from clouds. Good. He hoped it would stay that way.

They ducked down behind some jutting rocks at about 3 A.M. The rocks didn't provide complete shelter from the rain, but because of their angle, they cut it at least in half.

The clouds had rolled in at about midnight, and the rain right after. It hadn't been bad at first—the moon still shone through the clouds, and Slocum had a good bead on Apache's track—but then, about a half hour ago, the sky had darkened and the real rain had started pouring.

They were down into Mexico by now, and Slocum knew they were lucky to find this outcrop of rock. Any outcrop, really. Dugan was moving south, but this time far to the east of the mountains and through the flatness of the Sonoran Desert.

Slocum dismounted, then rubbed Red between the eyes. "For a horse with no spots, you're turnin' out to be pretty damn handy." The gelding whickered, as if it understood, then rubbed its face against Slocum's hand. Slocum grinned.

Wyatt was already pulling the tack off his horse. "Don't know about you, but this cowboy's stoppin' for the night."

"Good idea," Slocum said. He started to work at Red's tack. "He could be anywhere," he said, gazing south through the darkness and pounding rain. "Could be twenty miles, could be ten feet."

"Could be in Mexico City, for all I know," Wyatt said, pulling down the last of his tack. "I think maybe he's part witch, part devil."

"But mostly a bastard son of a bitch," grumbled Slocum. He was growing weary of trying to chase down the little prick.

And he was angry at him for making off with Apache.

And he was pissed at him about having to leave Mandy behind so that he could join Wyatt on this goddamn wild-goose chase.

He slipped the hobbles on Red, hauled his saddle back against a rock, put his slicker down, and sat. Who could tell what kind of crap Dugan was putting Apache through down there! And poor Mandy. He wondered where she was sleeping tonight, and with whom.

But his thoughts kept returning to Apache. It tore him up to think that one of the best horses he had ever owned was in the hands of that rat-bag murderer. "I'm gonna kill him this time," he said.

Wyatt didn't say anything, just kept trying to build a fire.

"This time, I'm gonna shoot him in the head and have done with it." His hands were balled into fists. "And if I can't do that, I'll beat him to death with my bare hands."

Wyatt sat back from his soggy kindling. "I'll help you, if we can catch him."

"Oh, I'll catch Dugan, all right," Slocum spat. "If it takes the rest of my goddamn life, I'll catch him."

Dugan was camped about ten miles off. He'd found a place where the rain couldn't get him—an overhang at the bottom of a rocky hill—and he'd tucked himself and Apache underneath just before the rains came. Now he found that he was too tired to sleep.

He hadn't bothered to strip Apache's tack. He wanted to be ready to ride at a moment's notice, in case those scumbag Earps—or Slocum—came after him. Those Earps! What a bunch of over-publicized, self-important gunhands they were! Why, that Morgan had walked right up next to his cell. As if he hadn't had something planned! Bang! Through the bars with his boot in his hand, and down went an Earp. Easy as pie. He only wished he could have chanced the noise of a gunshot and gotten rid of him permanently.

But he'd put him out of commission for the time being, at least. Enough time for him to steal down the street, get into the O.K. Livery, and swipe Slocum's horse.

He laughed softly. He wished he could have seen that bastard's face when he realized his horse was gone. Dugan bet he'd just pitched a fit! He picked up a rock from the ground and tossed it at the Appaloosa's croup. The horse snaked out his head, ears pinned, but Dugan was out of reach.

Actually, he'd found the Appy a troublesome ride. He balked half the time, and he kept trying to . . . escape, for lack of a better word. It was like he knew he'd been stolen!

Dugan shook his head. No, that was stupid. Horses couldn't think. Horses were dumb animals. Horses were dumb *stupid* animals!

So why did he feel like this one was . . . planning. Or something.

Well, he couldn't get away with anything tonight. Dugan had hobbled him and tied him and blocked him in so he couldn't go anywhere. Not without an act of God, that was. And Dugan figured God wasn't paying any attention. After all, He'd never shown any sign He was around before. Why should He show up now?

Miraculously, Dugan became aware that his eyes were growing heavy. It was about time. He needed to catch a few winks before he went any farther, if only to be aware of the horse's hijinks.

He yawned and laid his head back, pillowing it on his arm. He couldn't see the moon. All he could see was darkness and pouring rain. Somewhere, out there in the dark, a coyote howled, warbling a complaint about the weather. At least Dugan imagined it as a complaint.

Pack rats and mice would all be down in their burrows tonight and out of the rain, so the coyote's hunting would be fairly hopeless.

Everything was on "wait" tonight, including him. His eyes closed.

At last, he fell asleep.

Slocum, too, lay awake. He and Wyatt had at last chewed on the hardtack and jerky Slocum carried in his saddlebag, Wyatt having given up on ever getting a fire started, and now Wyatt was asleep, blissfully snoring beneath his slicker and blanket.

Slocum was dry, having hunkered under his slicker as well, but he could still find no rest. His mind still raced from Dugan to Apache to Mandy and back again. And then there was Will to worry about. Had he gone to see Doc Goodnight? Had he found out what was wrong?

Slocum turned over again. He couldn't get comfortable, damn it. He reached under his hip and dug a rock up out of the dirt, then cast it to the side. He thought, *I shouldn't be out here digging rocks out of my "mattress." I should be back up at the Oriental, playing a game of cards or upstairs, with Mandy.*

"Shut up," Wyatt slurred, startling Slocum. He hadn't said anything out loud, had he?

He watched as Wyatt shifted position, and listened while he muttered, "Got it, Virgil," under his breath.

Slocum felt better. At least he wasn't losing his mind. Wyatt just talked in his sleep, that was all, and Slocum relaxed again.

The rain had lessened, and right now, Slocum was waiting for it to come roaring up again. He wouldn't have been surprised at anything nature chose to throw at him at this point. But the clouds parted, letting a little starlight twinkle through. For the moment, anyway. And despite himself, Slocum took heart in that.

Just long enough for a big, fat raindrop to land square on his nose.

He was about to swear at it, but ended up chuckling instead—the first sign of mirth he'd given off since he'd heard about Apache being taken. "Well, shit," he said with a shake of his head.

He settled back down into the most comfortable position he could find and closed his eyes. He had to get some shut-eye before dawn, he told himself, as he actually began to drift off.

Red began to snore in concert with Wyatt, but Slocum barely heard it.

He was asleep.

12

The next morning, when Mandy woke up, she was not in her crib, but in Nellie Cashman's boardinghouse on Tough Nut Street. It took her a moment to remember how she'd gotten there.

Slocum. He was the man who'd made it possible. He'd pressed a fifty-dollar bill—a fifty!—on her before he left her with a kiss good-bye and told her he'd be back in a few days. Bless his ever-lovin' heart! It had taken her the better part of ten years to squirrel away nearly five thousand dollars—the amount she figured would allow her to quit the business and go someplace new, someplace where nobody knew her, someplace where she could make a new start. Slocum's fifty meant there were twenty-five less tricks she had to turn, and that she was almost there.

She was waiting on Slocum's return, hoping against hope that he'd feel just as generous a second time. Then, she vowed, she was out of this business for good and all. She'd go north. Maybe up to Prescott. She'd heard you could buy a nice house up there for under five hundred.

She had plans. She'd be a widow woman, she had decided. It wasn't like she could get a job. The only jobs that paid anything were being a schoolmarm and whoring, and she wasn't qualified to be a schoolmarm. But she could pose as a widow, and if she lived frugally . . .

She grinned wide.

Nellie Cashman, in whose boardinghouse she was staying, didn't take kindly to whores, but took very kindly indeed to those who had quit the trade and were trying to improve themselves, which was exactly what Mandy was attempting to do. And now she found herself in a clean, dry place with no holes in the walls and no rodents scurrying in and out, no drunkards wandering up and down, knocking on doors.

To say this was a much, much more pleasant place was a vast understatement.

She got up, dressed, and went down to the breakfast Miss Nellie included for boarders. And after a breakfast of fried eggs and potatoes, ham, toast and jam, and good piping-hot coffee, she went back to her room to stare again at her bankbook.

Five thousand and six dollars. And forty-two cents!

She was practically rich!

Slocum and Wyatt were up and awake, too. By noon, they had trailed Dugan to the place where he'd camped the night before. They stopped and had lunch under the cover of the overhang, mostly to avoid crouching in the mud, and Wyatt found enough dry kindling that they lit a small fire and had coffee.

They both appreciated it beyond words.

Wyatt had a few others to say, though. He took a sip

of his coffee. "Don't imagine we'll catch him till he hits Mexico City, at this rate."

Slocum flipped his quirley's butt end into the little fire. "Hope you're wrong, Wyatt. I got places to go, people to see. Things to do."

Actually, he didn't. He was just making conversation. You had to, with Wyatt. Come to think of it, with Will, too. He added, "How come you left your marshal's badge behind?"

"Couldn't be this far south if I was still wearin' it." Wyatt took another sip of coffee. "Thought you knew that, Slocum."

"Guess I did. Musta slipped my mind."

Wyatt prodded the fire, which was dying down to nothing. He shook his head. "Slipped your mind. Yeah, sure. I think you're just pokin' around for somethin' to say. Must be gettin' to be pretty slim pickin's."

Slocum chuckled. "Can't get nothin' past you, Wyatt."

"And let that be a lesson, buddy," Wyatt said, tongue in cheek. "Don't go tryin' it again. And I'll try not to be so boring." He stood up, then kicked out what little remained of their fire. "Hope three cups was enough for you. We're fresh out of heat."

Slocum got to his feet, too. "It was a right good start," he said. "Reckon I best go siphon some of it off before we get goin' again."

"Good idea," said Wyatt, and they wandered outside, splitting in opposite directions.

The day had gone hot, but clammy. Slocum didn't like it. Hot and dry was one thing, but this—his clothes sticking to his skin as if he'd just come out of the river, and the air feeling thick in his nostrils—didn't agree with him, not one bit. Wyatt rode alongside him like it was the most normal thing in the world, like nothing in the world could bother him.

Well, it might not affect a big-deal former U.S. marshal, Slocum thought, but it sure as hell was getting to him.

He tried to focus on the problem at hand, which was turning out not to be such a problem, after all. Apache's tracks were easy to follow through the mushy gravel and clay, and Slocum supposed that they'd set that way for a long time, once the air dried out. If it ever would. The gelding was balking on Dugan, he realized. Once or twice, Apache had even come to stop and tried to wheel around. They found signs in the broken sage where the horse had bucked. That Apache was some kind of horse, Slocum thought with a smile.

He had most likely recognized Dugan's scent from a few days back, when they first brought him into Tombstone, and that had been the only reason Dugan had been able to get on him in the first place. If he'd been a stranger, with a strange scent, he wouldn't have been able to get near the horse.

But he seemed familiar, so Apache had done his bidding. For a while. It was beginning to backfire on Dugan now. Apache wanted to get back to his herd, and his herd, it seemed, was Slocum.

Buck the bastard off, buddy, Slocum thought over and over. *Buck him off and come runnin' to me.*

He even pictured it in his mind, as if by seeing it, he could make it happen. But as they rode away the miles, there was no sorrel Appaloosa in sight. Only the signs of his passing.

"Damn you, horse!" Dugan shouted for the third time. Clinging to the single rein he'd managed to grip on his way out of the saddle, he stood up and brushed at his muddy trousers, one-handed, while he muttered curses under his breath and said, "I swear to Jesus, next town I come to, you're gonna make a short trip to the glue factory, you spotty-assed son of a bitch." He knew what town that would be, too. Calisto was just a few miles to the southeast.

Dugan tried to mount up again, but the horse swung its body around to the side before he could get his foot into the stirrup.

"Damn it!" Dugan roared, and lashed the horse across the face with the free end of the rein.

This time, Apache reared, kicked out with his elevated front hooves, and struck Dugan in the chest.

Dugan felt all the air go out of him in a rush, and tumbled backward. He ended sprawled on the desert floor, empty-handed and trying to catch his breath while he watched Apache gallop away, heels flying, toward the north.

Dugan was too angry to curse. Once he caught his breath, he stood up and watched the animal disappear. His face, unappealing to begin with, had taken on a ferocity seldom seen. If he could have, he would have pulled his rifle and shot that damn cayuse. But he couldn't, because his rifle was in the boot on the saddle.

Everything he had was on that mangy brute! Everything except what he had in his pockets and in his holsters, that was. Which wasn't much. He had his sidearm and the extra ammunition in his gunbelt. He had his pocketknife, a few matches, and his wallet. But that was about it.

Grumbling under his breath, he set out on foot for Calisto, hoping Slocum's damn horse would break a leg. Or two. Or maybe all four.

* * *

Something caught Slocum's eye. It was up ahead, on ground that, over the course of the afternoon, had started to undulate and now placed them on the wide floor of a shallow gorge. The uprisings hadn't become mountains yet. They had barely become hills. But Slocum could tell that they would gradually grow higher and higher as he and Wyatt traveled deeper south.

"Look!" he told Wyatt, and pointed at the moving speck in the far distance.

Wyatt reined in his bay and pulled out binoculars. He scanned the horizon. "I'll be damned," he said.

"What?" Slocum demanded.

Wyatt tucked his binoculars away. "It's your Appy."

They both lit out at a gallop.

When at last they caught up to the horse, he was proceeding at a walk, but halted when they rode closer. It was Apache, all right. He didn't look hurt, but he looked wild-eyed and disoriented. The men stopped a few feet off from him. Slocum got down out of the saddle and stepped forward.

"Easy, boy," Slocum said soothingly, his hand out toward the horse's nose. "Easy, Apache."

The horse snorted and tossed his head.

"It's all right. It's me, boy."

Apache pricked his ears, then laid them flat again.

Slocum could see now that the horse had been lashed across the face and carried a long welt diagonally between his eyes. Damn that Dugan!

Slocum held his ground. "C'mon, buddy, it's just me. Nobody here's gonna lash you across that pretty face. You're safe, boy, you're safe now . . ."

Eventually, the horse warmed up and stepped forward to nuzzle Slocum's hand. Despite Wyatt's irritation,

Slocum took the time to slowly walk the big gelding in a circle and make sure he wasn't limping, then offered him water.

Apache acted like he hadn't seen a drop for two days.

"I'll bet the bastard didn't feed you, either," Slocum muttered. He found the gelding's nosebag, slipped the bridle from his head and the bit from his mouth, and fitted on his halter. At last, he strapped on the nosebag, and the horse began grinding oats.

"*Now* are you done?" Wyatt carped.

Slocum looped Apache's bridle over his saddle horn, then clipped one end of a lead rope to his halter, and the other to Red's saddle horn. He climbed back up on Red. "Now I am," he said. You couldn't have wiped the grin off his face with a sponge and a squeegee.

"Don't s'pose we can barrel on ahead?" Wyatt asked sarcastically, watching Apache's jaws work.

"Nope," Slocum answered with a grin, and nudged Red into a walk.

Wyatt followed. "Why did I bother to ask?"

Slocum frowned quizzically. "You say somethin'?"

"Not a word," said Wyatt, shaking his head. "Not a goddamn word."

Late that afternoon, they found the place where Apache had bolted, and the same place where the trail carried on in boot prints instead of those of horseshoes.

Slocum was on the ground, staring at the boot prints. "He's goin' to Calisto," he said, raising his head. He pointed off farther south, on an angle.

Wyatt looked puzzled. "Calisto?"

"Keep forgettin' that you're a U.S. marshal," Slocum said and grinned. Wyatt hadn't had call to go into Mexico of late. If ever. Slocum stood up again. "Calisto's over yonder a few miles. Little bit of a town, mostly farmers. Used to be a hideout for Mexican banditos till a few years back."

Wyatt said, "Used to? Why do I have a feeling you had something to do with that?"

Slocum pulled off Red's empty feedbag, then remounted. "Oh, the townsfolk had a lot more to do with it than I did. They finally got riled up enough to do somethin' about it. Their problem, I mean."

"Yeah, sure," Wyatt said, and started his bay moving again, this time at a trot.

"Wish you'd quit pretendin' to believe me," said Slocum, goosing Red a little to the east. "You're gonna destroy my faith in the genuineness of your veracity."

Wyatt cocked a brow. "Ain't they the same thing?" he asked.

"Well, if you're gonna tear apart every cotton-pickin' thing I say . . ."

Wyatt held up one hand. "You ain't gonna change the subject by startin' an argument, Slocum!"

"Now, Wyatt, there you go again, puttin' all kinds of ulterior motives on me," Slocum said innocently. "All I was tryin' to say was—"

"Y'know," Wyatt broke in, "after we take care of this little problem, you oughta spend a few days in Tombstone. Have a few meals with us. Play poker with Doc and me. Go see some shows. You know, do the town up right."

"Wyatt, you're right," Slocum agreed, glad for the change in subject. "I surely ought to."

13

They rode into Calisto right at sunset. Wyatt followed Slocum, since Slocum seemed to know where he was going. Slocum had been silent for the last two hours, and Wyatt had followed his lead there, too. After all, Calisto was familiar territory for Slocum.

It wasn't much of a town. Barely a village, in fact. The town was built around a deep community well, with a market and a livery and a few shops ringing it, and only a few casitas studded the roads going in and out of town. The street around the well was dotted with chickens pecking the dirt and a few goats wandering about.

Slocum rode right up to a cantina and dismounted. Wyatt followed suit.

They waked through the batwing doors, and before they could say anything, a cry of "Slocum!" went up.

Suddenly, they were mobbed. Or at least as mobbed as they could be by seven patrons and a barmaid. The barmaid seemed to know Slocum *very* well. She curled up alongside him, saying, "Slocum, how fine it is to see you again." Somehow, by her tone, Wyatt suspected that it was a good deal more than "fine," and that she already had plans to show Slocum just how much more later.

"Good to see you again, Maria," Slocum said, slipping an arm about her shoulders. He greeted several in the small crowd by name. "Juan!" he said. "Tonio, Pepe!"

"Cerveza!" cried the one named Juan. "Cerveza for everyone!"

Wyatt wasn't about to turn down a free beer, so he went along with the crowd and sat down. Tonio was next to him, and he said, "Tonio? My name's Wyatt." He stuck out his hand. "Another Anglo come walkin' into town a little while ago?"

Apparently, Tonio didn't speak English, because his face twisted into an expression of puzzlement, and he said, "Qué?"

Wyatt said, "Slocum?" as the beers came and slid damply onto the table.

Slocum asked the same question of Juan, who nodded and translated for the rest of the crowd. It seemed Juan hadn't seen anybody, but two of the men and Maria jabbered away in Spanish.

"Gracias," said Slocum, after Juan had put it back into English. It seemed that Dugan had been here, all right, and he was still here, camped out over at the hotel.

"He was very tired," Maria said in English. "I bet he is asleeping already."

Smiling, Wyatt nodded and said, "Thanks." He'd bet that Dugan wasn't sleeping. He was probably across the street, aiming his pistol at the front doors of the cantina right this second. He turned to Juan. "You better tell everybody not to use the front doors for a spell. He's probably out there right now, watching."

Juan nodded and set into translating. Slocum looked

at Wyatt over his beer and said, "Smart. Same thing I was thinkin', as a matter of fact."

Wyatt grinned. "Ain't it always?"

"So, you wanna take care of this thing right now?"

"Might's well. We could have a couple more rounds, then dinner, and hope he gets more tired out—"

"But in the meantime he could change his mind and come for us instead."

Wyatt nodded. "You got it." He stood up. "Ready?"

Slocum rose, too. He was already eyeing the back door.

Wyatt pointed as they walked, as one man, toward it. "You go that way. I'm goin' to the right."

Slocum gave a quick nod and opened the door.

Both men stepped away from the opening, and once Slocum had determined that Dugan wasn't directly outside, they stepped through it and into the alley.

"Be careful," Wyatt whispered as they parted ways.

"You watch your ass, too."

Slocum crept down the alley, leaving Wyatt to go the other way. He came to the corner of the back of the building, paused, his back against the wall, and peeked around.

Nothing.

It was dark now. The sun had gone down while they were in the cantina, and around the corner the street seemed vacant. Seemed. That was the operable word. Slowly, Slocum stepped out, his gun drawn, and started forward toward the street.

They shouldn't have tied the horses out front, he realized as he crept forward. Dugan was enough of a rotten egg to shoot their horses if he didn't get them right off the bat. But it was too late now.

As he went slowly up to the street, Slocum could see that someone had lit the torches along the boardwalk, and there was just enough light for him to see that there was no one discernible on the street or in front of the squat adobe buildings. Which meant that Dugan was likely tucked away in a doorway, or in the mouth of an alley or a gap between buildings.

Or that Maria had been right. He could be asleep in his hotel bed.

But Slocum doubted it.

He came to the mouth of the alley, but paused before he stepped out onto the boardwalk. First, he took a good long look across the way. Nothing that he could see. He stepped out into the open, close to the building, and began creeping along the perimeter. A quick glance over his shoulder told him that Wyatt was in about the same place, slinking along in the opposite direction. Good.

When it came to bringing in a wanted man, you couldn't find better than Wyatt. He knew all the tricks of the trade—both his own and his quarry's—and he was quick and decisive. Much as Slocum himself was, although Slocum would never admit to the same.

He crossed the street at the far end of town at a dog-trot, then flattened himself at the front of the first building on the opposite side—a millinery and fabric shop, if he remembered right. Down across the well and the circle of buildings that surrounded it, he watched while Wyatt crossed the road, then disappeared into the shadows across the way.

A baby was crying somewhere, and Slocum froze until he located the sound's source. It wasn't coming from the hotel. It came from the little apartment over the dry goods store—the home of Mario and Constancia Martinez, Slocum thought. They'd had a baby, then. Well, good for them.

Not good for him, though. If Dugan had gone to bed, Slocum hoped he was a sound sleeper.

But he told himself again that Dugan wouldn't have gone to sleep, no matter how tired and sleep-deprived he was. More likely that he would have stolen another horse and hightailed it out of town.

Slocum began to move again, checking every hiding place, every nook and cranny, as he went, and beginning to think, more and more, that Dugan was gone. He was just coming up on the hotel when Wyatt yelled, "Over here!"

Slocum broke into a run and was at Wyatt's side in a few seconds. He yelled, "What?" as he skidded to a halt, and Wyatt began to laugh at him. Slocum scowled and asked, "What!" again.

Wyatt stopped laughing long enough to tell him that Dugan was gone. "Checked at the livery," Wyatt said. "Feller there speaks English, and he said that Dugan walked in this afternoon and actually bought a horse, then rode it on out of town."

"Bought it? Are we talkin' about the same Dugan?"

Wyatt nodded and fingered his mustache. "'Fraid so. So, you wanna head on out, or are you too pooped to pop?"

"I'd a lot druther sleep for the next week, but don't I reckon you're about to let me."

Wyatt smiled. "Reckon I am. I'm beat about to nothin', and the horses could use a decent rest, too. I vote we stay over and cut out early in the mornin'. All right by you?"

Slocum was delighted, but he just nodded his head in agreement. Now that he knew Dugan was gone, all the wire had gone out of his muscles, and suddenly all he wanted was to find a bed and climb into it. It didn't matter to him that Dugan was likely only a few miles ahead. The bastard was going to have to rest sometime, and Slocum was more than willing to shoot him while he slept.

Wyatt said, "I'll put the horses up, if you want. You can go get us a couple'a rooms." He hiked a thumb toward the hotel.

"Fine by me," said Slocum and turned back toward the hotel. "Oh," he said, turning back to face Wyatt. "Tell the folks at the cantina that they can come out now."

Smiling, Wyatt tipped his hat, then started back for the horses.

Slocum walked the other way, and was soon in the hotel's lobby.

He walked to the counter, toward a frightened-looking clerk, and opened his mouth.

But he had no time to say a word, because at about the same moment that he saw a gun barrel poking up over the counter, Dugan—Dugan!—rose up behind it, and with a short, barking laugh, said, "Good-bye, Slocum."

Slocum reached for his sidearm, but didn't have time to get to it before he heard a gun's roar, felt a heavy pain in his chest, and dropped to the floor like a stone.

Wyatt was just untying the first horse from the rail, having already called to the folks in the cantina that they could come out and that everything was fine, when he heard the shot. He whirled around, drawing his pistol, but saw nothing. No running forms, no gunsmoke, nothing.

"Hold up on that okay!" he called to the man just taking a first step from the cantina. Then he vaulted up onto his horse and galloped across the circle toward the place from which the shot, he was fairly certain, had emanated.

Once there, he vaulted off the bay while it was still galloping and hurled himself up against the front wall of the hotel. He landed with a bang, his pistol still drawn and ready, and yelled, "Slocum!"

There was no answer.

"Slocum!" he tried again. "Can you hear me?"

Again, no reply.

He got to his feet, quickly checked to make sure nothing important was broken, and flattened himself against the wall. And then he heard it.

Inside, a soft, barely audible voice was saying, "Señor Slocum! Señor Slocum! It is Ramon, Ramon Diaz! Señor Slocum, when you came before, you saved my little girl from the bandit's bullet, remember? Señor Slocum!"

Wyatt, still wary, edged to the side until he could peer in the window. What he saw disturbed him, to say the least. Slocum was lying on the floor, bleeding profusely from a bullet wound in his chest. He appeared to be unconscious. His head was in the lap of a youngish Mexican—Ramon Diaz, Wyatt assumed—who was trying in vain to revive him.

Since there were no guns—or other people—in the room, Wyatt made a dash for the door. A startled Ramon gave out a little gulp. His hands went into the air, dropping Slocum's head on the wooden floor with a loud thud.

"Who shot him?" Wyatt demanded.

"Señor Dugan. He was behind my counter. He said he would kill me if I moved or gave sign to the gringo who was coming!" Ramon was on a roll, and he couldn't seem to stop. "Such a big gun he had! I knew he would be trouble when he first checked in. Oh, Señor Slocum, wake up, wake up! Please don't die!"

Wyatt holstered his pistol and got down on the floor on Slocum's other side. He felt Slocum's neck for a pulse. It was weak, but it was there, thank God. "Where'd Dugan go?" he asked, cutting into Ramon's rant.

Ramon looked at him, perplexed.

"I said, where'd Dugan go?" he repeated in a louder voice.

"To . . . to the back," Ramon stammered, and pointed toward a back door. "His horse . . . his horse was tied there."

"Did he take off?"

"Yes, señor. I . . . I heard him gallop away."

"You got a doctor in this town?" Wyatt asked. Slocum didn't look good at all.

"*Sí*. You want I should get him?"

"Right away. Go!" He caught Slocum's head when Ramon scrambled to his feet, and as Ramon raced out the door, crying something in Spanish, Wyatt pulled a kerchief from his pocket and pressed it against Slocum's chest. He said softly, "Slocum, if you're half as smart as I think you are, you'll listen to your old buddy Ramon, and to me, too. Don't friggin' die, you got that?"

At just that moment, Slocum moaned softly and rolled his head back, although his eyes didn't open, didn't even flutter.

"That's right, Slocum," Wyatt said. "Stay with us, now, ol' buddy. Stay with us . . ."

14

Slocum woke the next day to find himself in a hotel bed, heavily bandaged across his chest, and relieved of his clothing. He squinted against the light from the open window, trying to remember how he'd come to be here. He could recall stepping into the hotel to find Ramon Diaz standing behind the counter, but there it ended. The rest was blank.

He tried to roll over to avoid the sun's rays, but when he moved, his chest and shoulder screamed in pain. He believed he must have made a noise, too, because the door opened and in walked Maria. She smiled at him before she turned back and called down the hallway, "Ramon! Tell the doctor and Mr. Wyatt that Slocum, he is awake!"

From far off, he heard Ramon's muttered, "*Sí*, Maria! *Bueno!*" and then the sound of bootsteps and a slamming door.

Maria came the rest of the way in and quickly stepped to pull the curtains.

"Thanks," Slocum said. His voice sounded off, even to him. "What happened, Maria?"

"You do not remember?"

He shook his head, but just a tad. Even that hurt.

"Last night you were attacked by the brute, Dugan," she said, with a look on her face that made it seem she was speaking of a deadly snake. "He left you for dead and rode away, to the south. Had it not been for Mr. Wyatt and Ramon, you would be dead." She sat on the edge of his mattress and picked up his hand. "Oh, my Slocum, I am so happy you are not dead. All of Calisto is rejoicing."

"Glad somebody's happy," Slocum mumbled, and tried to sit up. Pain stabbed his chest, and he groaned.

"No no, Slocum," scolded Maria like a mother hen. "You must not try to move yet. The doctor, he says so."

"Doctor?" He didn't recall any doctor. But then, he supposed he wasn't remembering anything very well. He glanced again at his bandages. Neat and orderly. Maybe they had called a doctor, after all.

"Yes. Dr. Ramirez," Maria said. She raised a brow. "He patch you up okay, no?"

Slocum managed a little smile. "He patched me up pretty slick, yes." He wished somebody would tell him what the doc had to patch him up *from*. Although he suspected it was a gunshot wound. It sure as hell felt like one, anyhow.

And then he remembered—Dugan, the gun, the sudden blast, and the staggering pain. Goddamn that Dugan! He balled his hands into fists.

Wyatt's voice boomed. "You musta sewed him up wrong, Doc. He looks like he's ready to slug you."

Slocum relaxed his hands. "Howdy, Wyatt." To the man next to Wyatt, he said, "And you must be Dr. Ramirez."

The doctor nodded. "At your service, señor."

Wyatt sat in a chair beside the door. "And he sure was at your service last night, buddy. Thought we were gonna lose you for a while there."

The doctor moved to Slocum's side, ushering Maria out of his way. He began unwrapping Slocum's bandage, after Wyatt leant a hand with helping Slocum to sit up.

Slowly, bit by bit as the doctor checked his wound and carefully rewrapped it with fresh dressings, Slocum put the whole story together. Dugan had shot him, all right, but as usual he'd missed his target—most likely, the heart. He'd shot high and to the right just far enough to avoid, as the doctor said, major organ damage.

Well, that was something to be grateful for, anyway.

As for the rest of it, Slocum wasn't so sure. Wyatt had just let Dugan go instead of riding out after him. He said that Slocum was hurt too badly to be left. Which Slocum supposed he might be grateful for, too, if he knew that Dugan's dead carcass was down in the stable. Which it wasn't.

But not that much time had passed, and Slocum had salted a whole lot of sleep away while Dugan had lost even more. He was beginning to see a bright side to this thing.

He said, "So, when can I ride, Doc?"

The doctor raised both brows in shocked surprise. "Ride? Are you sure you did not take a blow to the head, señor?"

He reached for Slocum's head with both hands, but Slocum jerked away from him—a movement for which he was immediately sorry. The doctor must have seen the pain on Slocum's face, because he followed with, "Señor Slocum, you will not be riding another horse for at least ten days. Perhaps longer."

"Doc, you don't understand. We're trackin' a killer. Bronc Dugan!" Slocum fumbled for the words to convey how dangerous Dugan was. "Um, *muy peligroso!* Or *mucho peligroso*. You don't want him runnin' loose in your country. I've gotta get back on the trail today."

But the doctor just shook his head. "Señor Slocum, this Dugan you chase has already done enough damage. Let others pick up where you left off. Stay. Rest."

"No. I'll be damned if I'll lay here and let you molly-coddle me while Dugan's out there, drawin' breath and free as a bird!" He attempted to swing his legs over the side of the bed and, miraculously, succeeded. It surprised him and the doctor both.

But the doctor blocked his path. "Señor, you must—"

"The only thing I must do, Doc, is go round up this son of a bitch. Wyatt, hand me my pants."

Wyatt pulled Slocum's pants out of the chifforobe and tossed them to him, while he said to the doctor, "I'm taking odds he won't even make it down the stairs."

"I heard that!" Slocum snapped. He struggled with his trousers and prayed to God that he wouldn't pass out.

"Sorry, pal," Wyatt said.

Dr. Ramirez stood, then threw up his hands. "I give up," he said. "What good is it to save a man's life when he is intent on taking it himself?" He stormed from the room with Maria—jabbering in Spanish—on his heels.

Wyatt shrugged, then helped Slocum get his britches on. "Shirt," said Slocum, panting from exertion. Wyatt pulled one from his saddlebags and helped him into it.

Slocum labored with the buttons, which kept shifting in and out of focus.

"Are you sure about this?" Wyatt asked. "Another day's layover won't bother me none."

Slocum knew he was lying. It would bother Wyatt plenty. So he said, "Shut up, Wyatt."

Wyatt shrugged. "Point taken."

"Good. I'd hate to have to rub it in any harder."

"You push any harder on it and you're gonna wind up on your ass," responded Wyatt. "Which is where you're headed right now." He took a few steps and caught Slocum just before he could tumble to the floor. "Just sit there for a goddamn minute and breathe, you crazy bastard. I'll be glad to set out after him today, but only with you breathin' and upright in the saddle, not strapped across it."

"Don't harp on me," Slocum growled. He grabbed hold of the mattress edge on either side of him, waiting for the strength to stand up.

It washed over him before he knew he had it, and he stood up rather suddenly, startling Wyatt, who jumped back a little and said, "Whoa, boy! You all right?"

"Fine," Slocum lied. "Where are my guns?"

Wyatt fetched them, and Slocum, one elbow on the dresser for balance, strapped them on. When he and Wyatt hit the bottom of the steps, Wyatt said, "Well, now that you've done that, I reckon you can do anything."

Slocum was seeing double, but clung steadfastly to the rail. "Now you're talkin' sense." *Don't pass out, don't pass out, don't pass out, you asshole!*

"In the interest of time, you sit yourself down whilst I go get the horses. You wanna ride the sorrel or the Appy?"

"The Appy. I'll pick the sorrel up on the way back, take him back up to Tombstone." Slocum made it to a chair and sat down more forcefully than he meant to. His chest was aching and burning, all at once. "Don't forget to fill them water bags, Wyatt. And find out what color horse Dugan's ridin'!"

* * *

Wyatt saw to the horses, tacked up the two of them, and talked to the stableman before he led his bay and Slocum's Appy back up to the hotel and went inside. He found Slocum just where he'd left him, except he'd passed out again.

He walked over and shook Slocum slightly. "Slocum? You in there?"

Slocum's lids popped open immediately. "Just restin' my eyes," he said without apology.

"Thought so," Wyatt said, although he didn't believe the big man for a second. He held out his hand. "C'mon. You'll do better once you're back in the saddle." This he believed with all his heart. He'd never met a tougher bird than Slocum, and he knew that once all Slocum had to worry about was sitting on his horse, he'd be fine. Or at least, he'd be better.

Of course, getting him up there in the first place was going to pose a problem.

Slocum grabbed hold of Wyatt's arm and hoisted himself up from the chair, nearly pulling Wyatt over. But Wyatt stood his ground, and soon the two of them were heading out front, toward the waiting horses.

Before he went to Apache's side, Slocum paused to rub the horse's head and neck, greeting him. "It's all right, buddy," Wyatt heard him say. "Papa's back. You're all right now."

Slocum went to Apache's side, gathered his reins, and put a foot up in the stirrup. While Wyatt waited, ready to catch him when he fell, Slocum mounted effortlessly.

"Well, I'll be damned," Wyatt muttered beneath his breath, then said, "You okay, Slocum?"

"Fine as frog's hair," came the reply, and Wyatt, grinning, shook his head. He walked around and swung up on his horse.

"Ready?" he asked.

"If you are," Slocum replied. "He went south?"

"Yeah."

"Then let's go find him." Slocum reined his horse around and headed toward the southbound road out of town.

"Oh, yes *sir*," Wyatt said with a grin.

Slocum pushed them both up into a jog. "You weren't ever in the military, were you, Wyatt?"

Wyatt shook his head. "No. Why?"

"Because I wasn't ever a 'sir.' Just a sniper."

Well, that answered a whole lot of questions that Wyatt had never asked. He just said, "Oh," and rode on.

15

They stopped at about noon to rest the horses and get themselves some grub. Slocum was glad to learn that Wyatt hadn't wasted his time in Calisto: he'd bought them a ham, a couple loaves of bread, a stack of tortillas, and a roast chicken, along with a sack of Mexican wedding cookies.

The horses were seen to, and Slocum settled back with a drumstick in hand. Wyatt had simply ripped the roasted hen in half, and handed Slocum his chunk of it.

While Slocum polished off more than half of his half, Wyatt brewed coffee over a small flame, then handed Slocum a mug. He said, "I take it you're feelin' better?"

Slocum nodded. "Yeah." He took a big bite out of the breast. Actually, he was feeling pretty damned good, and he looked over at the Appy. "The outside of a horse is good for the inside of a man." He'd read that somewhere. The author obviously knew what he was talking about.

"Well, if you get to feelin' punk, I found out what Maria was jabberin' to the doc about when he left,"

Wyatt said, and reached into his pocket. He pulled out a small paper packet. "Heroin," he said. "It'll fix you up right away. You're supposed to wait until bedtime to take it, though."

Slocum nodded. "All right. Maria bring that to you?"

Wyatt stuck the paper back in his pocket. "Uh huh," he said before he took a sip of his coffee. "She said that he says it's the latest thing."

Slocum nodded. "Don't believe I've had that kind before. Glad he didn't send opium. Can't stand that stuff."

"You sound like you tried it."

"Anybody who's been shot up or busted up or carved up as many times as me? I've had more docs throwin' more kindsa 'get well pills' at me than I can count. Or remember." His teeth ripped into the wing.

Wyatt smiled. "I reckon you have, reckon you have."

They rode out again a few minutes later.

They had come out into a desert strewn with boulders, like giant grains from God's saltshaker, Slocum thought. The desert was green from the recent rains, the cactus fat with water, and the occasional tree had upright branches and glossy leaves. There were mountains to the west of them, but not ahead, and Dugan's horse's hoofprints showed clearly in the still damp gravel of the desert floor.

They had still not come to a place where Dugan had camped, and it had Wyatt in a tizzy.

He stormed. "Jesus Christ! Doesn't the man need to rest? Ever?"

"Calm down, Wyatt," Slocum said. "He's gotta stop and sleep sometime."

"Yeah, but when? The stinkin' bastard's not human if you ask me."

"I 'magine he's been sleepin' in the saddle a bit," Slocum offered. "Now that he's got shed of Apache, I mean. If he'd tried to pull that on Apache, he'd have woke up halfway back to Tombstone. Ain't that right, fella?"

He patted the horse on his neck, remembering to use his right hand. He'd done it with the left the last time, and instantaneously, pain had shot through his shoulder and chest like bolt lightning, honed to a razor's edge. This time, it wasn't nearly so painful, although it still hurt. But he could live with it at least.

"Well," Wyatt said, "he's still movin' his ass too fast for me. He gets down to Mexico City, we're gonna have a helluva time pickin' him up."

"True," said Slocum. "But we'll get him before then."

Wyatt raised a brow. "And what makes you the fortune-teller, all of a sudden?"

"Ain't no magic to it. I'm just watchin' his tracks. He's slowin' down."

Wyatt leaned forward in his saddle and peered at the ground ahead. The tracks were growing closer together. "You're right," he admitted.

"Hold it!" Slocum hissed, and Wyatt reined in next to him.

"What?"

"There's our man, right there."

"Where?" asked Wyatt, scanning the horizon.

"Closer. Right near that big boulder up ahead. See his legs stickin' out?"

Wyatt stared a little longer, then muttered, "Well, shit, Slocum. What now?"

Slocum carefully scratched the back of his right hand with his left. He said, "We could go ahead and ride in there, but Dugan's tricky. Might be lying there with his guns drawn, just waitin' for us to do that. On the other hand, he might be sleepin', in which case, if we go creepin' up there, we might just wake him up and suffer the same consequences." He stared Wyatt straight in the eyes and smiled a little. "You choose, Mr. Former U.S. Marshal."

Wyatt thumbed back his hat, shook his head, and softly swore. "Shit," he said. "Maggoty shit on a pie plate."

Slocum raised a brow. "That bad?"

"Damn right it is. I figure we could hide out behind a rock of our own—if'n we had one—and wait him out. You sure ain't gonna be no good at tippy-toein' up there. You can hardly walk."

"Rub it in, why don'tcha?" Once again, Slocum peered at the boulder behind which Dugan was hiding. "Wyatt, how big you reckon that rock is?"

Wyatt thought a moment, then said, "Gotta be mayhap seven feet or more. Can't even see his horse's ears over it."

"That's what I was thinkin'. What you say we ride on up there, close to the backside of the rock as we can get, then split up. You go round the foot end, I'll go round the other. He can't shoot us both, 'less he's got two guns. And even then, he's liable to miss at least one of us."

"Good thinkin'."

They began to move forward, very slowly.

"One thing," Slocum whispered.

"What?"

"When we get around that rock—if we get around that rock—and we're faced off on either side of him? Don't shoot me."

Wyatt slapped a hand over his own mouth to hold the laughter back. They both moved forward, eyes alert for any signs of movement, ears keen for any sound out of the ordinary—and Wyatt still tittering behind his hand.

When they were about ten feet out from the boulder, Dugan's legs moved. Not much, but enough that both men stopped dead.

"He awake?" Wyatt whispered.

Slocum signaled with his hand for Wyatt to hush up. Dugan's legs showed no further movement, so after a while, Slocum signaled them forward.

They split up, with Wyatt going west and Slocum going east to surround the rock. When Slocum crept around the eastern side of the massive boulder—and the back end of Dugan's horse—he found Wyatt, gun cocked, standing over a sleeping Dugan.

Asleep, he didn't look dangerous at all. He just looked like a sleeping man, maybe one that's had too much to drink. Slocum knew different, though. He knew that Dugan was just sleeping off all those hours and hours of no sleep.

He crept forward and carefully slipped Dugan's Colt from its holster, then tucked it in his own belt. Dugan didn't rouse. Slocum took a step backward and looked at Wyatt. Although his first instinct was to simply plug Dugan and get it over with, once he drew his pistol, he just stood there. Eventually, he looked over at Wyatt and shrugged.

Wyatt returned the gesture. It seemed that neither one of them had it in him to shoot a sleeping man.

After a moment, Wyatt kicked Dugan's boot and said in a loud voice, "It's the end of the trail, Dugan. Wake up."

Dugan woke slowly, and Wyatt had to kick him again. He finally opened an eye, got one look at Wyatt, and his hand immediately slapped his empty holster.

"Sorry, Dugan," Slocum said a little smugly. "You been disarmed. Didn't nobody ever tell you that sleeping into the afternoon ain't good for you?"

. Apparently, if somebody had, Dugan hadn't listened.

He pounded the dirt with his fist and shouted, "Damn it, anyhow!" He turned toward Slocum—who was presently leaning, with his right shoulder, against the rock— and asked, "Won't you ever die, you bastard? You got more lives than a barn cat!"

"I do my best," Slocum drawled lazily. Actually, his chest and left shoulder were killing him, and he wanted nothing more than to switch places with Dugan, just to lie down for a few minutes. But Wyatt had other ideas.

"Stand up," he barked at Dugan.

Dugan struggled to his feet and stood there, glaring at them.

Slocum said, "Your call, Wyatt."

"How'd you bring him in the first time?"

"Over his horse."

"Good idea. We'll do 'er again. Keep your gun on him, Slocum. I'll tack up his horse."

They made it back to the place they'd stopped for lunch, and decided to stop there. Although the sky held no clouds and there was no scent of oncoming rain in the air, Wyatt and Slocum agreed that this was the place. Four smaller boulders were ringed in a crude circle, which might provide some shelter should they need it, and the vegetation had dried some more, providing Wyatt with plenty of kindling and wood to construct a fire.

They saw to Dugan first. The ropes that bound him to his saddle were released, and they dragged him, still hog-tied, to sit, leaning against the smallest rock.

Slocum had warned Wyatt about Dugan's mouth, so he remained gagged. He wasn't very happy about it.

Slocum was having a tough time moving, now. It seemed as if even the slightest gesture sent arcs of pain through his chest and shoulder. It must have shown on his face, because, in the middle of slipping the tack off his bay, Wyatt came to where Slocum was slouched against the rock opposite Dugan's and slipped the little packet from his pocket again.

"Not all at once," he cautioned. "Doc said all of it would kill you. Take a third and hold it under your tongue."

Slocum nodded, but before he dosed himself, he asked, "How strong is this stuff, anyhow?"

"Strong enough to knock down even a big ol' redneck like you, ol' buddy. But not right away, I reckon." He slid his horse's halter on and hobbled it. "Imagine you'll stay with us long enough to put away some ham."

"That's good news." Slocum poured about a third of the powder straight from the packet into his mouth. And gagged. He held the powder in his mouth though, letting it dissolve under his tongue before he said, "Damn it, Wyatt! Tastes like shit!"

Wyatt shrugged innocently. "It's what the doctor ordered, Slocum. Now, why don't you sit down and take it easy?" He moved to loosen Apache's girth. "I'll get supper on soon's I take care'a this spotted horse a' yours."

Slocum slid down the rock, letting his back take the pressure, until he landed in a sit. "Hobbles in the saddlebag," he said to Wyatt. The words came out slightly slurred. Was he already feeling a little dizzy?

16

The next morning found them on the trail again. Wyatt figured that they'd make Calisto late this afternoon, even if they couldn't gallop. He was concerned for Slocum. The heroin had knocked him out, all right—he'd passed out halfway through his ham dinner, and Wyatt had spent the night intermittently napping and snoozing, waking every few minutes to come full awake and level his pistol at Dugan. Dugan had gotten a full night's sleep, though. Like Slocum, he had spent the night without moving a muscle. Slept like the dead, as a matter of fact.

Good thing, Wyatt thought. He'd better get used to it. He was going to be taking a dirt nap for eternity about a day after they got back to Tombstone.

And Slocum was bearing up pretty well for a man who was supposed to be bedridden for a week or ten days. He couldn't yet pick up his saddle, but he'd managed to stand up by himself this morning. That had surprised Wyatt. He thought it had surprised Slocum, too.

Then again, last night, while Wyatt was off in the

brush, peeing while he kept an eye on Dugan—who was similarly engaged—Slocum had simply rolled on his side and let loose a stream next to the fire. He did it in a spot where nobody had taken up residence, but still, it wasn't like Slocum.

Wyatt supposed it was the medicine. If it had that big an effect on Slocum, Wyatt imagined once word about it got around, there'd be a big call for it.

They stopped around noon and grabbed some lunch, during which time Wyatt saw fit to leave off Dugan's gag a little longer than usual. This only served to give Dugan a chance to spew out more expletives at both Slocum and him, so he retied the gag, even though Dugan hadn't finished his lunch. Slocum only snorted his amusement.

In fact, Slocum was less communicative than usual, in fact he was now indecipherable. He'd talked some last night at the campfire. But not more than two words since then. As Wyatt remembered, he'd asked for coffee and said, "Good ham" and "Don't forget to pee, Dick-wad Dugan," before he'd passed out. Not the most elevating conversation.

And today, he'd just grunted. Or snorted. Wyatt wasn't sure you could count those as words, but considering it was Slocum, he did.

And now it was nightfall, and Wyatt began to recognize the road that would take them into Calisto. Juan, from the bar, was on the street, and he was the first to greet them. "Señor Slocum! Señor Wyatt!" he shouted. "Have you killed your desperado?" He spat near Dugan's horse's feet and swore an oath in Spanish.

And then Maria poked her head out of the cantina and let out a squeal of delight. She ran toward them, laughing and thanking the Lord that Slocum wasn't dead. Slocum didn't even have a word for her. Just a nod and a silly smile. By the time they had ridden to the livery, they had attracted quite a crowd. Well, quite a crowd for Calisto. Wyatt guessed that there were fifteen people in their wake.

After he pulled down Dugan—and stopped the crowd from kicking the helpless man who'd shot "their" Slocum—Wyatt managed to pry Slocum off Apache. Juan helped him get the horses put up—and promised to stand guard over them through the night. Wyatt checked on Red, who was happy as a clam and glossy as a housecat, having been pampered by half the town just because he was Slocum's horse.

Wyatt shook his head. It must be something to have a whole town consider you their savior. But then, it'd sure be a hard thing to live up to.

Ramon came over from the hotel, and he and Maria helped Slocum get up to his room, while Wyatt saw to Dugan. He got a double for him and Dugan, and tied Dugan to the bed as firmly as he could, then cuffed him for good measure.

Dugan signaled that he wanted his gag taken out, but Wyatt said, "No dice, Dugan. Don't want you disturbin' the other guests with that mouth a' yours."

Dugan muttered something back at him—likely filthy—then settled into silence.

Wyatt ordered dinner from the cantina, left Ramon to guard Dugan, and went in to see Slocum. Wyatt found him sitting on the edge of the mattress, staring at the paper packet he'd just pulled from his pocket. Slocum looked up at him. "I'm s'psed to take half this tonight, right?"

Wyatt, surprised by this outburst of conversation—almost an oration, all things considered—simply nodded.

Slocum tipped the packet back, into his mouth. Immediately, his face twisted. "Tastes like shit."

"You said that last night."

"True today, too," Slocum said with a lopsided smirk.

"Ordered you some dinner. Should be over in slap time. Hope you like enchiladas."

"Almost as good as steak," Slocum mumbled, and Wyatt wondered if he'd still be awake when his dinner was delivered.

"May I enter?" Wyatt looked up at the voice. It was Dr. Ramirez.

"Sure," Wyatt said. "Was about to send for you anyhow."

"How is our patient?" Ramirez sat on the edge of the mattress and began to unbutton Slocum's shirt. Slocum gave him no fight, just an evil look.

"He's doin' just grand," Wyatt lied. But then, he wasn't really lying, he realized. Slocum was doing very, very well, all things considered.

"Good. He hasn't bled through his bandages. Always the good sign," the doctor muttered. He began to snip away at Slocum's wrappings. "If you would help me in a moment, Señor Wyatt?"

Wyatt moved to the other side of the bed, and when the doc was ready, they helped Slocum sit up so they could get him out of his shirt and the rest of his bandages. Even Wyatt could tell that the wound was healing rapidly and cleanly. He could give the doc some of the credit, but he gave most of it, although silently, to Slocum. He *did* have more lives than a barn cat!

Later, after the doc had re-bandaged him with fresh wrappings, Slocum ate his dinner. He seemed to enjoy it, or what of it he ate. Once again, he fell asleep before he finished. Wyatt figured he'd gotten more of it down this time, though. He quietly gathered Slocum's plate and coffee cup and left for his own room and dinner—and Dugan's—closing the door behind him.

Dugan was in a foul mood, as usual. The first thing he said after Wyatt took the gag off was "He dead yet?"

Wyatt shoved his dinner plate at him. "Shut up and eat."

"You're just givin' me a spoon to eat enchiladas with? And how 'bout untyin' me?"

"Nice try," said Wyatt around a mouthful of Spanish rice. Then he repeated, "Just shut up and eat."

That night, in the cantina, Wyatt relaxed with a beer. He'd left Juan to babysit Dugan this time, giving him orders to not remove the gag, and not to let him take a piss. Wyatt had let him empty his bladder into the chamber pot before he left, so he figured he could just sit there until he got back. And with the gag in, he couldn't use any fancy talk on Juan.

Or course, he didn't figure Juan would fall for it. The whole town was still mad at Dugan for what he'd done to Slocum. Mad? Mad wasn't the word for it. They were ready to hang him. *Never let a bunch of Mexican farmers get on your bad side,* Wyatt told himself, even though the same fate awaited Dugan once they got him back up to the states. Now, that'd be a hanging Wyatt would admire to see, and he wasn't much for spectating. He imagined Morgan was looking forward to it, too, as well as Virgil.

His brothers were "by the book" lawmen.

Well, he supposed he was, too. Elsewise, he would have just shot Dugan back down where they picked him up.

And maybe they should have.

Maria came over to his table and sat down opposite him. She asked, "Slocum, he does well?"

"He's doin' all right," Wyatt answered with a curt nod. "That medicine Doc Ramirez gave him is workin' like a charm. He's out like a light."

Maria said, "It makes me glad that he is doing so well. He will recover?"

Wyatt nodded again. "Yeah, he'll do fine." He hoped to hell he wasn't lying.

He had another beer with Maria before he said good night and made his way back over to the hotel. He was dog tired and looking forward to sleeping in a bed for a change.

When he got back to the room and had said good night to Juan, he got Dugan up and let him have a last shot at the chamber pot for the night, then tied him up again and lay down on the other bed—fully dressed, gun in his hand and pointed toward Dugan.

"Don't try anything, you son of a bitch" were his last words before he dozed off to sleep, off and on, throughout the night.

Slocum woke the next morning all by himself, got up, and used the chamber pot. He checked his bandages in the mirror over the bureau. The bandages were still fresh, and when he had tried to move his arm earlier, he hadn't felt like hot knives were stabbing him. Cold knives, maybe. But it was a vast improvement.

He found his shirt and put it on all by himself, gathered up what gear Wyatt had brought up for him, and opened the door before he realized that he didn't know where Wyatt and Dugan were. He'd be damned if he was going to go up and down the hall rapping on every door, so he went to the head of the stairs and called down.

"Ramon? Ramon, you down there?"

Ramon stuck his head around the corner and into view at the bottom of the steps. "*Sí?*" Then, delighted, he said, "Señor Slocum! You are better?"

Slocum grinned. "Better, yes, Ramon. Where's Wyatt and the prisoner?"

"*Nombre* 107, Señor Slocum." He puffed out his chest a little. "I aided in the guarding. So did many here."

"Well, thank you, Ramon," Slocum said. "Thank you very much."

"*De nada*," said Ramon with a little bow.

Slocum nodded at him and Ramon saluted in reply. Slocum chuckled and waved his hand. His right one. He still didn't have much faith in the left.

He walked back up the corridor to room 107 and rapped at the door.

Wyatt stuck his head out. "Slocum!" he said, surprised and obviously happy. "You're up!"

Slocum grinned back. "Feelin' some'at better, too. How's Dugan?"

"Well, he's awake anyhow. C'mon in."

Slocum entered the room to find Dugan sitting on the edge of his bed, looking cranky as hell and still bound. He was still gagged with the same bandana, too.

Wyatt said, "You reckon we can trust him far enough to cart him to the cantina for breakfast?"

Slocum replied, "Reckon we're gonna have to, 'cause I seem to have built up a powerful hunger durin' the night." He looked at Dugan. "You promise to be a good boy?"

Behind the gag, Dugan sneered at him.

"Well, best untie his feet then. I ain't gonna carry him," said Wyatt, and bent to the task.

They packed in a good breakfast at the cantina. Slocum even had a beer, seeing as how they weren't leaving until after nine. Juan, having run across the way, had their gear and horses all ready for them when they arrived at the stable.

"Thanks, Juan!" called Wyatt. "Wish I could get this kind of help up home." He laughed when he said it. He got Dugan's feet hog-tied—with little struggle from Dugan—and got him up over Red's back and secured. They sold his horse back to the livery, and Slocum insisted that Wyatt pocket the money.

He said, "They don't pay marshals enough, and he ain't got no kin, far's I know."

Wyatt shrugged, but finally pocketed the forty dollars. Although he grumbled about it.

Slocum got on his horse by himself—well, with the aid of a mounting block—and they waved good-bye to Calisto and its residents and headed north.

"I don't figure we'll make Bisbee tonight," Wyatt said as they rode along. "You're likely not up to gallopin' yet."

Slocum, full of eggs and tortillas, shook his head. "But try me after lunch. Might be up to a good run then, maybe."

Wyatt raised his brows. "We'll see," he said. "We'll see."

Slocum cocked his head to the side, but simply rode on.

17

They stopped at noon without incident, and after lunch Slocum pushed Apache—not into a full-fledged gallop, but an easy lope. He was so accustomed to Apache's rhythms that he fell right into it and found it as easy to ride as the walk they'd been traveling at.

They had plenty of water, so they paused at the river only long enough to let the horses drink, then scrambled across it, going northward, up into the States. Well, the Territory, anyhow. Slocum saw the unspoken relief wash over Wyatt's face the moment they rode up on the northern bank.

Wyatt dipped his fingers into a pocket and pulled out a badge, which he proceeded to pin on his shirt, under his vest.

"Thought you left that with Virgil," Slocum said.

"I lied," said a cheerful Wyatt, pulling his vest over the nickel star.

"Feeling better now?" Slocum smiled.

"Some'at. As a matter of fact, yes."

Slocum laughed. "Once a lawman, always a lawman."

"Reckon so," Wyatt said, and laughed.

They pushed the horses into a lope and headed north, toward Bisbee.

They didn't make it to Bisbee that night. Wyatt had been right, although Slocum was loath to admit it. But they got to within five miles of the town before they made camp.

Throughout the day, Slocum had continued to improve. He supposed that was the way things went. With him, anyway. Fresh wounds most always felt worse than they actually were, but the pain eased off pretty danged fast. He'd had several doctors remark that he was a quick healer, and they'd been right. Of course, they hadn't been around when he'd suffered some of his worst injuries. They never were, were they? But he supposed that most of the time, they were right. He did heal up quick.

He still wasn't himself, though. But he would come around. He had no doubts.

He didn't get out his heroin as early as he had the night before. First off, he didn't need it yet, although it sure did help him sleep and he was planning on taking it eventually. Second, he and Wyatt were having a good talk. Wyatt seemed to be enjoying it, too, although Dugan didn't seem to care either way.

Wyatt talked about growing up in Iowa, Slocum spoke of his boyhood in the South. Wyatt talked about his first wife, about losing her, and about going west, to Kansas. For his part, Slocum spoke of the War and its aftermath. As it affected him, anyway.

Finally, at about nine, Slocum had used up all his energy, and he pulled the packet of powder from his pocket. "Believe I'll take my poison now, Wyatt," he said, and proceeded to pour the last of it into his mouth. It tasted terrible, like always, and like always, he couldn't help but make a face while he waited for it to melt under his tongue.

"Crap!" he said, finally, and washed the taste down his throat with the last of his coffee. Wyatt had brought along a goodly supply of Arbuckle's, which Slocum greatly appreciated. The cup he had just drained was his fifth of the night. It was also the first supper he'd finished in a while.

The heroin kicked in almost immediately, and he felt a relaxing warmth move through his body. "Y'know," he said, "I never realize how bad my chest hurts till it stops. Ain't that somethin'?"

He must have slurred his words, because Wyatt just looked at him quizzically.

"Never mind," he tried to say.

"Lemme get your blanket spread out," Wyatt offered generously.

"Get it myself," Slocum tried to say, but it came out more like "Gemmyfelf." He gave up on talking. All he wanted to do now was lie down and fall asleep.

Wyatt had his place ready before he knew it. Slocum crawled toward his blanket and fell into it, head pillowed on his saddle.

Slocum dreamt hard that night, and his dreams started out pleasant enough. He dreamt about Mandy, about her hair the color of sunshine, about her pert, full breasts and tiny waist, and the appealing swell of her hips. He dreamt that she was going down on him, and it felt so good, so magically good . . .

But then—he wasn't sure how—he found himself on the streets of Tombstone, found himself there, fully dressed, with Mandy's scent still clinging to him, and realized that the streets were empty of pedestrians, and that the only other person present as far as the eye could see was Bronc Dugan.

Dugan drew his gun and Slocum drew his. Dugan's aim was apparently better from afar than it had been up close, because just as Slocum felt heat and pain spreading through his chest, he saw Dugan fall to his knees. Dugan went the rest of the way down, but Slocum realized his angle of sight was changing. He was watching from above now, watching the whole thing play out like a stage show, seen from the highest balcony on an impossibly large stage.

He watched people come running from the buildings on either side of the street—it was Allen Street, he recognized it. Some ran to Dugan, kicking away his gun, but most ran to—him? Was that him down there, lying on his back in the dirt? How the hell—?

"Slocum?" Wyatt's voice. "Slocum? You all right?"

Slocum opened his eyes. The lids felt heavy, like there were bags of cement holding them down, but he gazed up at Wyatt. It was dark. "What happened to the light?" He shifted his head. Rocks instead of buildings. "What happened to the town, your town?"

Wyatt smiled. "You were dreamin', buddy."

Slocum let his head loll back. "Where are we?"

"We're a few miles south of Bisbee. We'll be in Tombstone tomorrow, Slocum, if we ride hard." Wyatt's brow furrowed. "That musta been one helluva dream. You okay now?"

Slocum wasn't a bit sure, but he said, "Fine. Just fine, now. What time?"

"What time is it now?" Wyatt pulled out his pocket watch. "'Bout three-thirty. Way too early for you to be shoutin' out loud and wakin' folks up."

"Shoutin'?" Slocum replied groggily. "Sorry."

"No harm done," Wyatt said, smiling a little, and pointed at Slocum's chest. "You can put that smoke-wagon away, now."

"Huh?" Only then did Slocum realize he was gripping something, and that the something was his pistol. His finger was on the trigger, and he eased it off. His brow furrowed. "I didn't—"

"No, you didn't fire. But it was pointed straight at Dugan." Wyatt relieved him of his gun and stuck it back in his holster.

Slocum sighed. "Thanks, Wyatt." He felt his lids begin to close again. "Sorry," he repeated.

He felt Wyatt's hand on his shoulder. "S'all right, Slocum. Just get back to sleep. I'll wake you when . . ."

Wyatt kept talking, but it was lost on Slocum. He had fallen asleep.

Slocum woke on his own the following morning at about six, when the sun was just over the horizon and the desert was coming to life. Wyatt was already awake, and somewhat more mobile, and he grinned at Slocum from across the fire. Slcoum smelled coffee brewing and carefully sat up.

He was amazed at how his shoulder felt! It was almost as if he hadn't been wounded at all, although he realized that part of this magic had been worked by the heroin, which hadn't completely worn off yet. He took advantage of the situation, though, and got to his feet. He wandered off to take a piss.

He was just buttoning up his britches when he smelled

the ham frying. It was a lucky thing Wyatt was a good campfire cook, or Slocum would have starved to death these last few days. He walked back around the rock to find Wyatt not only frying up the ham, but the last of their eggs, as well. Slocum smiled. He was hungry!

"Coffee'll be ready in a minute," Wyatt said. He smiled. "Can you hang on that long?"

"Think I could hang by my teeth from a rope," Slocum joked.

Wyatt laughed.

"Want me to take him for a short walk so he can piss?" Slocum asked, indicating Dugan.

"Already done," said Wyatt. "Breakfast's ready." He shoveled ham and eggs onto three plates, removed Dugan's gag, then handed out the plates. Dugan took his without a word, and Wyatt paused.

"What the hell's wrong with you this mornin'? No commentary? No insults? No complaints?"

Dugan, his hands bound, just continued eating.

"Cat's got his tongue," said Slocum. The ham and eggs were great, as was the coffee. There was a covered skillet still on the fire, though. Hopefully, Slocum asked, "Those biscuits I smell?"

"Bingo," Wyatt said around a mouthful of ham. "Ready in a second."

Once they finished eating and had the dishes cleaned and the fire extinguished, it was time to saddle the horses. Slocum tacked up Apache himself, after he gave him a quick brushing down. Wyatt finished his bay and Red at about the same time.

"Been thinkin', Slocum," he said as he moved Dugan toward Red. "Think we'd best let Dugan ride upright today."

Slocum raised his brows. "Why you thinkin' that?"

"'Cause we're gonna go through some rough country today. Don't wanna deliver him with a head fulla burrs."

Slocum didn't answer for a minute. If it was him, he'd throw Dugan over his horse and damn the burrs and sage. But Wyatt had his badge back on, and besides, Slocum trusted him. So, flying in the face of his better instincts, he said, "Sure. But tie his feet to the stirrups, and don't untie his hands. And don't bridle the horse."

Wyatt, who had already made a makeshift halter from loops of Red's lead rope, said, "Fine by me," and bent to untie the ropes around Dugan's boots.

Dugan behaved himself, mostly because Slocum had a gun pointed at him during the whole procedure. Once his feet were free, Dugan was allowed to climb up into the saddle. Wyatt quickly roped one foot into its stirrup, then walked around Red and took care of the other one, while Dugan took a good grip on the saddle horn.

Slocum holstered his pistol and mounted up. So did Wyatt. And then they moved out, Slocum letting Wyatt take the lead while he trailed behind Dugan.

He was taking no chances. He figured that Dugan could get away easy, even roped in place. He could lean forward and push the lead rope over Red's ears. He'd have no trouble controlling him, even with no headstall on, if he was good enough with his legs. Slocum didn't know how good a rider Dugan was, but you could never be too careful. In addition, Dugan could pull up one stirrup at a time, if no one was watching him, and get his legs free.

As they moved steadily northward, Slocum's gaze fairly drilled a hole in Dugan's back.

"Don't try it, you rat-bastard," he growled under his breath. "Just don't try anything."

"You okay back there?" Wyatt shouted.

Slocum waved a hand, although his eyes were still on Dugan's back. "I'm fine."

"You need to stop, just holler."

Slocum nodded. "Will do, will do."

18

They bypassed Bisbee, rather than going through it. This was Wyatt's decision, but Slocum agreed with it. Dugan was hard enough to hang onto without adding a whole lot of street traffic to the mix.

So far, Dugan had minded his p's and q's, but that didn't mean that Slocum relaxed any. His shoulder and chest were paining him again—probably as much from the stress and strain he was putting on his whole body than from anything else. Keeping an eye on Dugan was no easy job, especially for a man in his condition.

Additionally, he found himself fussing over where he'd get his next dose of heroin. Now, this wasn't like him at all. Longing for a woman or a steak or a drink, that was more like him. But yearning after medicine? Not like him at all.

He took a chance and fumbled for his fixings pouch, then rolled himself a quirley, all while never taking his eyes off Dugan. He lit the quirley and took his first drag. He was right. Smoking did calm him down.

At least for a while.

Before he knew it, Wyatt was stopping, and Slocum reined in Apache just in time to avoid running into Red's backside. Wyatt untied Dugan's feet, enabling him to dismount, and Slocum held a gun on him while Wyatt built a fire and started the coffee. Slocum could have bypassed the coffee in the middle of the day, but Wyatt insisted.

And, as Slocum told himself, the marshal's the marshal.

Wyatt broke out the last of the ham, along with the leftover biscuits from breakfast, and they ate a cold lunch. Dugan seemed pleased to have the ropes off his feet. At least, he sat cross-legged by the fire, something he couldn't do when he was tied, and Slocum almost felt sorry for the way they'd handled him before.

Almost.

But not quite.

The pain in his chest wouldn't let him.

Wyatt had no such difficulty. After lunch and the ensuing cleanup, he saddled Dugan just the way he had in the morning, roping his legs to the stirrups. Although it seemed to Slocum that he wasn't quite as careful. But then, Slocum wasn't doing so well himself, and he might have looked away for just a second. Longer, maybe. His chest was aching like a bastard.

It won't be long now, he told himself. *It won't be long before we get to Tombstone. It won't be long before I can lie down.*

Despite his best intentions, Slocum fell asleep in the saddle. He hadn't wanted to, had never guessed he would, but he did.

He woke to the sound of scuffling, of hoofbeats galloping, of Wyatt crying out, "Slocum! Slocum, wake up, dammit!"

He came full awake to find Wyatt on the ground, try- ing to get up, and to see the backside of Red, carrying Dugan, as he galloped over a small hill.

What had he allowed to happen? "Need help?" he quickly asked Wyatt.

And Wyatt just pointed and shouted, "Go after him!"

Slocum didn't hesitate.

He showed his heels to Apache, who seemed to know the chase was on, for he bolted so fast that he nearly ran out from under Slocum. He headed for the rise over which Dugan had disappeared.

But how the hell had he gotten loose? Had he slipped his feet free? Had he got the makeshift halter off the horse's head? Had he somehow gotten his hands free?

It didn't matter now.

Nothing mattered except getting Dugan back. Slocum would be damned if he was going to chase all over hell and gone for that son of a bitch all over again!

He crested the hill. It dipped down into another small brush-dotted valley, studded with boulders and upthrusts of ragged rock. And he couldn't see Dugan. Couldn't see him anywhere.

But he could see the signs of his passing. He kneed Apache forward again, but this time at a pace not so urgent. Dugan could be lurking behind any of the larger rocks down there, waiting to jump him.

And he was in no shape to be jumped.

He came to the lowest part of the valley. Dugan's tracks still headed onward, to the east, and he followed, all the while cursing under his breath. After less than ten yards, he saw something out of the ordinary and halted abruptly, slipping off Apache effortlessly.

What had stopped him was the sight of Red's backside, sticking out just slightly from behind an upthrust of rock. As he watched, the horse moved out of sight, as if he were being led or ridden. But he couldn't be being ridden—the rock was only about six and a half feet high at its tallest point, and if Dugan had been on him, his torso would have shown over the top of it.

So the bastard had somehow gotten his feet free and slid from the saddle. Now all Slocum had to worry about were his hands, and whether or not he'd managed to snag himself a weapon. The last thing was the one that had Slocum the most concerned. Capturing Dugan, on the loose but unarmed, would be like trying to stick a greased bobcat into a gunnysack, barehanded. But if he was armed?

Lord, have mercy!

He heard the brush rustle behind him and turned back to see Wyatt, mounted but holding a bandana to a wound on his head, riding down toward him.

"Find him?" Wyatt shouted.

Slocum grimaced, then signaled Wyatt to shut up and get off his horse. Then he pointed toward the place where Dugan was hiding. "He's back there," he whispered, once Wyatt got close enough.

"Whatcha waitin' for?" Wyatt asked, perplexed.

"For you to get here." When Wyatt just stared at him, he went on, "Because he's got his feet unbound, or he couldn't have got down off the horse. Which means he's likely got rid of his wrist ropes, too. And I can't remember whether or not there's a spare pistol in those saddlebags of Red's. Can you?"

Wyatt just stared at him for a long time before he said, "Well, horseshit."

"Yeah," concurred Slocum. "That, too."

Wyatt said, "I'll go right."

Slocum nodded curtly.

Wyatt left his bay behind and carefully crossed to the next rock on the right, which was about twenty feet over. He slipped beside it, nodded to Slocum, than called out, "Bronc Dugan. This is Deputy U.S. Marshal Wyatt Earp. If you're smart, you'll give up now, Dugan!"

"Fat chance!" came the reply—and along with it a slug that zinged off the rock in front of Wyatt.

Wyatt ducked down and cried out, "Crap!" Then, "Where'd you get that goddamn smokewagon, Dugan?"

Dugan didn't answer. But he took another shot at Wyatt when the top of the lawman's hat peeked over the rock. Fortunately, it wasn't a part of the hat his head was in, because the slug sent it flying.

While Wyatt scrambled to retrieve his hat, swearing the whole time, Slocum was deep in thought. Something had been bothering him for days about Red's tack. Something that he hadn't put his finger on until just now. If there was a pistol in the bottom of one saddlebag, and apparently there had been, it was an old Colt, one Slocum kept just in case. Except this time, it had been "just in case" for Dugan.

But Slocum couldn't remember how many cartridges he had left for it. There'd been five in the gun, and part of a box. A very slim box, as he remembered, practically empty. Four more? Five?

Any way you looked at it, it was a bad deal for Slocum and Wyatt. Dugan had enough to reload, and it looked like he was going to keep shooting as long as he had ammunition.

Slocum figured Dugan could keep them pinned down until dark, if he had a mind to.

He signaled Wyatt to draw Dugan's fire again.

Wyatt shot him a pained expression, but he did it. Slocum kept his gaze on the rock Dugan was firing from behind.

Sure as anything, when Wyatt fired, Slocum saw the top of Dugan's head pop up, just momentarily, over the top of the rock. He was a little north of where he'd left Red, down where the upthrust of rock was maybe four and a half or five feet tall. Slocum nodded, and whispered, "Now you're gonna get it, you escape-happy son of a bitch."

He signaled to Wyatt again. Wyatt, who seemed to be catching on to his plan, nodded and fired over his rock again.

Dugan's head popped up, just like clockwork. And Slocum fired at the same instant.

Dugan never returned his fire. His head slipped downward, and he was silent.

"Did you get him?" Wyatt shouted.

"Think so. Hold on a second." Slocum pursed his lips and whistled one shrill, short blast. "Red!" he called. "C'mon, boy!"

He heard some shuffling of equine feet, and then Red stuck his head around the side of the rock and whinnied, as if he didn't now what to do. *Makes sense,* thought Slocum. Red had been carting Slocum, then nobody, then Dugan for several days. He didn't know who to answer to.

Besides, Slocum and Wyatt were behind the rocks, hidden from view.

Slocum took a chance and stepped into the open. "Red?" he said again and held out his hand. "C'mere, old buddy."

The horse came to him right away, and Slocum made a fuss over him, rubbing his forehead and stroking his neck. "Good boy. Good Red. You had yourself an adventure, didn't you?"

The horse whickered softly.

Wyatt came out, too. "Don't seem to have suffered any damage."

"No, he's in a fine fettle," said Slocum happily. "But mebbe we oughta check out Dugan."

"Got ya." Wyatt trotted off to the rock opposite them, and a few moments later, he shouted. "Nice shootin'! Got him square between the eyes!"

Slocum relaxed. In fact, all the air went out of him, and he slid to the ground.

19

When Wyatt came back to fetch Red, Slocum was flat on the ground. At first, Wyatt thought he was dead. Could Dugan have fired without their realizing it? But then he saw Slocum's chest gently rising and falling, and realized Slocum was sleeping! Sleeping at a time like this?

Wyatt shook his head. He would never, so long as he lived, understand some people. He bridled Red, then grabbed his reins and led him back to where Dugan's body waited.

He later admitted, just to Virgil, that he gave the body a good kick, just in case. Dugan had escaped so many times that he didn't trust him to actually be dead, despite the bullet hole in his forehead. But he still didn't move, didn't take a breath, didn't pull up a gun.

And so Wyatt heaved him up onto Red, roped him into place, and led him back to where Slocum lay sleeping with the other horses. He knelt down and shook Slocum awake.

"You in there, Slocum?"

Slocum grumbled something indiscernible.

Wyatt shook him again. "Hey, you big ol' bounty hunter! Wake up!"

Slocum opened one eye, then, from instinct, brought up his hand—with the cocked gun still in it. He aimed it straight at Wyatt's face until his head seemed to clear, and he lowered his right arm, saying, "Sorry, Wyatt. Force of habit, I reckon."

"Reckon you're right," Wyatt said, although he didn't smile until Slocum had holstered his Colt. Whether he knew it or not, Slocum was a lethal weapon.

Slocum stood up, although somewhat creakily, and nodded toward Red and his baggage. "He dead?"

Wyatt nodded.

"You sure?"

Wyatt grabbed Dugan's hair and lifted his head. The bullet hole was still there, in the center of his forehead. Wyatt let go, and the head dropped back down. "Deader'n a doornail."

"Finally," said Slocum, with no small amount of relief.

"Let's get him back to town."

"I'm with you on that."

The two men and their cargo rode into Tombstone after dark. They rode straight to the sheriff's office, and Wyatt dismounted at the same time the door opened and Virgil stepped out.

"I'll be double-dogged!" Virgil shouted, and held out his arms to hug his brother.

"He'll be double-dogged, and he don't know the half of it," Slocum said, and dismounted. The pain had lessened as the day wore on—especially after Dugan had been killed, and at the moment, Slocum was barely feeling any pain at all. He wondered how Will was doing, then felt bad for not having given him a thought for so long. *Well, if he went to see Doc Goodnight, he's probably right as rain by now,* Slocum thought. He swung down off Apache, and was immediately reminded of his wound.

He must have had a pained expression, because Wyatt turned away from his brother and asked, "You all right?"

"Yeah," Slocum said. "Slug hole's just actin' up a mite, that's all." He stuck out his right hand. "Howdy, Virgil. How's Morgan doin'?"

"He's up and around," Virgil said, "and drivin' everybody crazy. You'd think he'd just been attacked by a passel of Apache!"

"That Morg!" Wyatt said, and broke out laughing.

Slocum, grinning, followed them inside the office. He figured that once they got the amenities seen to, and the paperwork, he was going to go have himself a bottle of champagne. A whole one, all to himself. He'd been feeling hot, and he was also thinking about that bucket of ice they served it in.

Morgan was in the office, and when he saw Wyatt and Slocum he called out, "Welcome back, you two ol' hound dogs! Glad to see you, glad to see you!" He, too, hugged his brother, then shook Slocum's hand. "Did you get him? Did you bring that rattlesnake back?"

"Got him," Wyatt said, then poked his thumb toward the door. "He's outside over a sorrel horse, deader'n a swamp log."

Wyatt and Slocum pulled out chairs facing the marshal's desk. It was good to be sitting down again, and on something that wasn't moving. Morgan got them all some coffee while Virgil sat down behind the desk.

"So, what happened out there?" Virgil asked as he accepted his cup. "And what happened to you, Slocum?"

"Dugan," Slocum said, and took a sip of his coffee. Wyatt's was good, but there was something about stove-cooked coffee that was better. He took another drink. "Shot me in the chest."

"That rat-bastard," muttered Morgan.

"His aim was off some, though," said Wyatt. "Didn't manage to hit anything important, just tear up some muscle. And Slocum wouldn't have any truck with the doc's orders. He was supposed to be laid up for a week or ten days, but we were off the next mornin', trailin' that horse's butt."

Virgil's brow creased. "You mean he got away from you *again*?"

Wyatt shook his head. "No, no. We'd just caught up with him in some little Mex town. What was the name of it, Slocum?"

"Calisto," Slocum said, thinking that maybe he'd put off the champagne for tonight. He was already feeling drowsy in addition to achy.

"That's right," said Wyatt.

He kept on talking, but Slocum began to lose the thread of the conversation, and then whole chunks of it. He didn't know how much time had passed when he came full awake to find Wyatt's hand on his shoulder.

"C'mon, ol' buddy," Wyatt said. "We'd best get you to the hotel, I reckon."

Groggily, Slocum stood up, then said, "Wait. Gotta take care'a my horses."

"Don't worry. Morgan's already seein' to it."

Slocum nodded, although he wasn't too sure about Morgan. But he supposed it was better than nothing. He allowed Wyatt to walk him to the Oriental, where Wyatt got him a room.

"No charge," he told the clerk. Slocum had forgotten that Wyatt was part-owner of the place, and nodded his thanks as Wyatt guided him up the stairs. "Anythin' else you need? Food? Female companionship? Beer?" Wyatt asked. He let Slocum slide down to the edge of the bed.

Slocum said, "Nope, not tonight. Just wanna sleep."

Wyatt said, "Okay, ol' man. Good show out there."

Slocum touched the brim of his hat. "Right back atcha. And thanks again for the room."

"Anything you want, all you gotta do is ask."

Slocum nodded. He was so weary that he couldn't even think of taking off his boots, let alone his guns. It all seemed like too much work. And his chest was aching like a son of a bitch. He wished he hadn't run out of heroin.

He raised his right hand. "Thanks, Wyatt. G'night." And then he thought of something. "My guns . . ."

One hand on the doorknob, Wyatt waved the other. "Don't fret 'bout it. Reckon Virgil can make an exception for you this time."

"Thanks," Slocum said.

And then Wyatt bid him good night and was gone. Slocum didn't even take the time to straighten out on the bed. He just lay back—fell back, really—and he was asleep, feet on the floor.

When he next awoke, he found Doc Goodnight bending over him.

"Well, he's awake now," the doc said to someone behind him.

Then Will stepped into view, grinning like a fool. "Welcome back, stranger!"

"How long?" Slocum asked. As his eyes adjusted, he could see that it was mid-morning. He just didn't know what day.

"You were infected," Will said, still all smiles. "You been out three days, you big ox."

Doc Goodnight nodded. "Lucky you got back to town when you did, Mr. Slocum. If that infection had gone on much longer, the Earps'd be out there on Boot Hill, diggin' you a hole right next to Bronc Dugan's. You're one lucky bastard, if you don't mind me sayin' it."

"Been called worse," Slocum said, with a hint of a smile.

"You shoulda seen your bandages when we peeled you outta them," said Will, shaking his head.

"Smelled 'em, more like," added Doc Goodnight. "What kind of a butcher'd you see down there?"

Slocum had liked Doc Ramirez. He'd thought he'd done a good job, and he told Doc Goodnight so.

"Good job, my ass," the doctor grumbled. "He's the one who gave you that heroin, too, ain't he?"

Slocum nodded. "So?"

"Don't you trust that stuff," warned the doctor. "I don't. Seen folks get hooked on it, get hooked on it worse than those people down at the opium tents." He scowled at the wall. "Stay away from that stuff, you hear?"

"I hear," said a dutiful Slocum. Whatever Doc Goodnight had been doing for him the last few days, it had worked wonders. He had stopped feeling feverish, and the pain in his chest had focused in, to a point much smaller and finer than before. Much less painful, too.

There was a tap at the door, and Will went to answer

it. He couldn't hear the questioner, but he heard Will say, "Oh, he's a whole lot better. You wanna see him?"

He led Mandy around Doc Goodnight, and she immediately left Will behind to crouch on the bed next to Slocum. Her arms went around him somewhat gingerly, and she whispered, "You're alive, you're alive!"

He chuckled. "Hope to kiss a pig, I am."

When she pulled her head back and looked at him, puzzled, he added, "Nothin' personal, baby. Can't tell you how really great it is to see you again." He brushed a kiss over her forehead, and she replied by kissing him on the mouth, long and hard.

"Easy, baby," he said with a chuckle, once he had the use of his lips back. "I'm still tender."

"He's right, Mandy," came Doc Goodnight's voice. "Don't go doin' anything that'll make him pull out those new stitches."

"Wouldn't hurt him for the world, Doc," she said, running the back of her fingers down Slocum's cheek. "He's one in a million, our Slocum."

"You can say that again," Will stated. "Slocum, me and Morgan been taking real good care'a your horses. If you ever get down to the stable, you'll find 'em in a fine fettle."

"If I *ever*?"

"Aw, hell. You know what I mean. I'm just real glad you're among the livin', Slocum. You shoulda seen all the pus and stuff that came out!"

Mandy wrinkled her nose.

Doc Goodnight was putting on his jacket again. He nodded. "He's right, Mr. Slocum. You were in one hell of a mess."

"It's just plain Slocum, Doc," Slocum said. "Mr. Slocum was my pa."

Goodnight nodded quickly and straightened his coat. "Take it easy, Slocum. I mean, real easy. You're not allowed to get out of that bed until tomorrow, midday. And that's if you don't have any more problems with the wound. You do, you get hold of me right away, all right?" He handed Slocum a card, engraved with his name and address.

When Slocum looked perplexed at such a fancy, engraved business card, the doc said, "We're not all living in the Stone Age, Slocum. Good day now." Medical case in hand, he stepped out into the hall and closed the door behind him.

20

"Well!" said Will. "Guess he told *you*!"

Slocum grinned and tightened his grip around Mandy's waist. It felt good to be himself again. He said, "Really? Three days?"

Will nodded. "Thought you were gonna kick the bucket for a few days there. It's sure good to talk to you, pal."

"Good to be hearin' you, too," Slocum said, and smiled. "You go see him yourself?"

Will nodded. "Said it was . . . Hell, I can't remember. But he gave me some pills, and I'm a whole lot better now."

Will was his same old self, and Slocum was glad. To Mandy, he said, "Sorry, honey, but I think I'd best lie down again."

She smiled. "With or without me, baby?"

"Sorry, Mandy. I'm just too damn tired." He was, too. His lids were drooping already.

"That's all right, Slocum," she purred. "In case you

need something to do later, when you wake up, I brought you some things to read the other day." She pointed to the bed stand, where newspapers and a few dime novels were stacked.

He grinned sloppily. "Thanks, honey. Thanks a lot." He pushed himself back on the bed and lay down, pulling his legs up after him. Only then did he notice that he had been stripped down to his long johns, and those had been peeled down to his waist. He was still bandaged across his upper chest, although the bandages were fresh.

Mandy kissed his forehead, whispering, "Feel better soon, big man," and was gone before he knew it.

"I'll be gettin' along, too," said Will. "I'm just down the hall, if you remember. Same room."

Slocum nodded, and his head felt like lead. How could just sitting up for a few minutes take so much out of him? He didn't know. He just wanted to go to sleep.

His eyes closed and he heard Will exit the room. And then he heard nothing. He was asleep.

Within three more days, Slocum was up and around, and actually walked down the stairs by himself. He stopped in the bar and ordered himself a beer and a thick roast beef sandwich, and spoke a few words with Wyatt, who had just come in to take his shift at the faro table.

He stopped by Slocum's corner first, though.

"You're up!" he said as he pulled out the chair opposite Slocum.

"That I am. Not exactly fit to fight off my weight in bobcats yet, but at least I'm standin' and sittin'."

Wyatt laughed. Then his face turned serious, and no one could look more serious than Wyatt when he wanted. That long, droopy mustache made it seem like his frown was headed for boot level. He said, "We buried Dugan almost a week ago. Nobody came. Big surprise."

"You check to make sure he didn't dig his way out?"

Wyatt grinned. "Morgan's been up there three times since. I think he's checkin'."

A chuckle escaped Slocum. And it didn't hurt! He said, "Good for Morgan. I'd be goin' up there myself, if I was him. Even if I was me."

Grinning, Wyatt shook his head and scraped back his chair. "I'll bet you would. I'd better get my ass to work. See you later!"

Slocum had noticed the faro table was busy before, but when Wyatt sat down to deal, an even bigger crowd gathered. Slocum suspected it wasn't his deal that pulled in the rubes, it was his company.

When Slocum finished his sandwich and beer a few minutes later, the bartender informed him that his money was no good at the Oriental. Wyatt's orders.

"Thank you kindly," said Slocum to the barkeep, who smiled back at him.

"What the boss wants, the boss gets," he informed Slocum before he glanced over toward the faro table. "Boy, he sure does get folks to buck that tiger on a regular basis." He gave his head a shake.

"Sure does," agreed Slocum. "He surely does."

Slocum's next stop was the livery. He found Apache and Red turned out in the corral, both looking like they were a couple of statues, they were so clean and sleek and shiny. The Earps had done a helluva job, that was all he could say. And everything free at the Oriental? If he hadn't been in Tombstone, and it hadn't been the Earps, he would have figured that there had to be a catch somewhere.

But he had his money, and he'd brought in his

quarry—twice. Plus, Dugan—despite his bad aim and his even worse temperament—was now underground, and wouldn't bother anybody anymore.

"Hey you!" a voice called. "The marshal know you're carryin' them guns?"

Slocum turned to find himself confronted by the stable hand, a boy of about seventeen or so with a very annoyed expression on his face.

"As a matter of fact, he does," Slocum said, keeping his tone even. This kid had best figure out where he was and who he was confronting. For many in Tombstone, killing a man was as easy as asking him to pass the salt. "You'd best watch your tone, kid," he said. "Not everybody's as forgivin' as I am."

The boy scowled at him but said nothing further. Slocum had given him a quick visual once-over already, to make sure he wasn't carrying. That's all he'd need right now, to have some idiot kid gun him down, just to get a reputation. He went ahead and checked the horses Dugan's gang had stolen from the folks over in Monkey Springs. They looked fine, too. He took a peek at Duster, too, so long as he was out there. Once again, everything was just fine.

He left, but not before he called out to the belligerent stable boy again. "Nice job, takin' care'a my horses. I appreciate it."

The boy looked like he was going to smile, but he managed to cut it off midway, and scowled instead. It seemed like he wasn't going to give an inch to Slocum.

Slocum opened his mouth to say something else, like *Relax* or *Take it easy, kid.* But he closed it again without uttering a word. The kid had a burr under his blanket, all right, and Slocum wasn't going to volunteer to remove it for him.

Well, no one would ever accuse Slocum of being a humanitarian.

He left the livery and slowly strolled down the road, to the bank. Allen Street was lively even at one in the afternoon. As Slocum walked along, painted women beckoned from second-story windows, and the sound of heavy-handed piano playing competed with the occasional somewhat lighter touch on the keyboard, and the even more occasional nickelodeon. The sidewalks were crowded with cowhands, miners, and the gussied-up gambler or two. They were all sorts of races, from white to black to Indian to Chinese to Mexican. Most had been relieved of their guns, but some either hadn't seen the signs or didn't give a rat's ass.

Slocum figured it to be the latter in most cases. These boys didn't look like they took to arbitrary rules any too kindly.

Slocum guessed the kid down at the stable hadn't been up this way today. If he wanted to pick a fight, he'd undoubtedly find a lot of takers up here.

Slocum decided to cross the street and walk back up to the Oriental on the other side, which wasn't nearly as rife with bars and pleasure palaces and such. It was, in fact, like being in a whole other town. Here, the watering holes and dens of iniquity had been replaced by assayers' offices, millinery and dressmakers' shops, notions shops, tobacconists, dry goods and feed stores, and so on.

He reminded himself to ask Wyatt if there was some kind of a law that had gone into effect to split Allen Street that way or if the separation had been voluntary.

He almost ran into Virgil, who was just stepping out

of a tobacconist's shop. "Whoa!" Slocum said, and grabbed Virgil's shoulder to keep from running into him.

Virgil said, "Well, as I live and breathe! Slocum's back from the dead!"

"Almost, but not quite," said Slocum with a laugh. "I trust that you ain't seen Wyatt yet?"

"Nope. Reckon he's up at the Oriental, dealin', while I been doing my marshal duties."

Slocum tipped his head across the street and down the road. "Bunch a' boys down there with iron on their hips. That part of your marshal duty?"

Virgil snorted. "Reckon the boys from out at the Clantons' place are in town again. Well, I'll wait for Wyatt or Morgan. They respond better to a group."

"Know what you mean," said Slocum. "Say, you wouldn't happen to know where I could find Mandy, would you? A little blonde, 'bout—"

Virgil cut in. "Oh, everybody knows Mandy. She's stayin' over at Nellie Cashman's these days. Comin' up in the world, I guess."

Slocum raised a brow. He knew Nellie Cashman from up north, in the mining camps, and he knew she didn't allow soiled doves, at least those that were plying their trade, under her roof. Unless they were in a peck of trouble, that was. Miss Nellie had a soft heart.

"Where's Miss Nellie's?"

Virgil pointed down the street. "It's on Tough Nut, down a block or so."

"Thanks, Virgil." Slocum tipped his hat. "Best get some ready-mades while I'm here."

Virgil nodded. "See you. Stay alive."

"Do my best." Slocum opened the shop's door and went in, accompanied by a tinkling bell.

He bought his ready-mades—three packs—a box of

sulfur-tips, and went on his way. He'd been thinking about Mandy, thinking hard. And he was pretty sure that he'd come up with something, something that was good for both him and her, something that would give them both a lot of pleasure.

He turned the corner at Tough Nut and proceeded down to Miss Nellie's. The Russ House, she was calling it, but her name was on the sign, too. An old miner sat outside on one of the sidewalk chairs, smoking a pipe. "Lookin' for Miss Nellie, are ya?" he asked in a gravelly voice.

Slocum stepped up on the walk. "Kinda. Lookin' for one of her boarders."

"Got quite a few, quite a few," the old man rasped. "Who you lookin' for, 'xactly?"

Slocum couldn't see that it was any of his business, but he figured to humor the old coot. "Lookin' for a lady named Miss Mandy. Just moved over a few days back." A few days! Had it only been a few days? "Mighta been more like a week," he added.

"Oh, sure," said the old coot, this time with a cackling laugh. "I know Miss Mandy. Used to live over by the cribs." He pointed toward the alley where the working girls kept shop. "She's retired, or so she says. Shame, ain't it?" He looked at Slocum as if he expected an answer.

"Yeah," Slocum said. "A real shame. I guess. She here now?"

The old-timer shook his woolly head. "A real shame. Yup, she's here now. Room number seven. And you treat her right, you hear? She's outta business!"

Slocum smiled. He was glad she had defenders at the Russ House, even if they didn't pose much of a threat. He tipped his hat, then walked inside.

The lobby was homey. A painting of Nellie Cashman hung across from the front desk, next to an old coat tree, and Nellie herself was behind the desk.

"Can I be of help to you, sir?" she asked before she took a closer look. "Slocum?" And then the question went out of her voice, and she cried, "Slocum! My God, they were tellin' me you were dead as a tinned herring!"

He grinned at her, grinned wide. "I'm gettin' a lotta that lately. Hope you ain't disappointed."

She came out from behind the desk and threw her arms around him. He'd forgotten what a tiny thing she was.

"Disappointed?" she said, squeezing him tight. "By Holy Mary and all the saints, it's delighted I am to see you walkin' and talkin'!"

"Back atcha, Miss Nellie," he said with a laugh. "Good to hear the old sod drippin' off your tongue, too!"

"I'm still remindin' you of your sainted mother, then?"

"That you do, lass," he said. "That you do. I'm lookin' for one of your tenants, Miss Nellie."

She let go of him and backed up a step, still smiling. "And who would that be?"

"A little blond thing, name'a Mandy."

"Now, Slocum, you wouldn't be plannin' on any funny business under my roof, would you now?" she said, pretending to scold.

"And damn my soul to eternal perdition? Miss Nellie, you know me better than that," he said, pretending to be hurt.

"Aye, that's the trouble, John Slocum," she said with a laugh. "I *do* know you! Number seven, and no monkey business!"

Slocum tipped his hat, said "Yes, ma'am!" and went down the hall.

21

"That's the deal, Mandy. Take it or leave it." Slocum sat across from Mandy—he on the bed and she in the chair—and he was grinning like an idiot.

"But Slocum—" She looked shocked, and she could barely get the words out.

"Don't be silly. It's a good deal. In fact, it's a great one, if I don't mind sayin' so myself. You got a bank account here in town?"

"Well . . . yes," she said warily. "But—"

"Good!" he said, and took his feet. "And no 'buts' about it." He held down his hand. "You comin', little bird?"

"I . . . I guess." She took his hand and rose to her feet. "But Slocum, I don't understand! How did you—"

"Get it?" he said, finishing her sentence. "It's all legal, trust me. And I can't think of a better way to get rid of it."

He led her to the door, down the hall, past a curious Nellie Cashman, and outside. "Let's us go to the bank, Mandy!"

He'd been thinking about it long and hard, and had finally settled on a conclusion. Fair and just, to his mind. He knew that Mandy had been saving for a very long time—ten years, in fact—to get the money to retire, a thing that she was about to do. But he had a mind to let her retire in style.

When they came to the bank, he transferred five thousand dollars into her account. "Now it's yours, no ifs, ands, or buts." He watched as she signed the form with shaky hands. He'd done a good thing, he thought. A very good thing.

The teller handed her back her bankbook, which now showed a total of $9,998.42. It was a goodly sum of money for anyone to have, Slocum thought. Enough to buy her a house and furnish it, enough to live out the rest of her life in comfort. Modest comfort, but comfort nonetheless. She'd never go hungry, he figured, or have to work again.

She was staring at her bankbook like it was from another planet. "Slocum," she said slowly, "I can't find words."

"Not necessary," he said with a quick wave of his hand. He walked her to the door, then out onto the sidewalk.

They talked for a few minutes—not about the money, because he had banned the argument from their conversation, but about where she wanted to go to settle down. Prescott seemed to be high on her list. She'd never been there, but she'd heard good things about it.

"You'd best talk to Will," he said. "He lives up there, seems to like it."

Just then, he caught a glimpse of someone he halfway knew—the surly youngster from the livery. The boy was coming across the street, leading a fully tacked-up horse. And the kid was wearing a Colt pistol on his hip.

He looked like 150 pounds of trouble.

Slocum moved Mandy down the walk a ways, then told her to go on back home. "I'll join you in a little while," he said, and swatted her backside.

She moved away, wagging her finger at him. "No funny business at Miss Nellie's, now . . ."

He grinned. "I know, I know." He watched her make her way down Allen, and turned around just in time to see the kid tie his horse out front of the bank. The boy stood there a moment, nervously fingering his vest, then took a deep breath.

He stepped up onto the sidewalk, then into the bank.

Slocum was on him like white on rice, catching the door before it closed behind him, and entering just in time to see him draw his gun and hear him say, "Take it easy, everybody. This here's a stickup."

Slocum drew his pistol, flipped it quickly around in his hand, and cracked the kid over the back of his head, knocking him out cold. The kid slipped to the floor without ever cocking his gun.

"Somebody wanna go get the marshal?" Slocum asked, holstering his unfired gun.

All around him, everyone was frozen—tellers and customers alike. But finally one of the tellers "unfroze" and suddenly came zipping out from behind his cage. "Thank you, sir!" he said as he came across the room. "Thank you very much!" He was out the door, and Slocum could hear him crying, "Marshal! Marshal Earp! Sheriff Behan!" Apparently he was calling on everybody he could think of.

Just as well, Slocum figured.

At Slocum's feet, the boy groaned softly. Slocum

quickly moved to kick the gun out of his reach. In the far corner, a man was using his bankbook to fan, to little avail, the face of a large woman who had fainted.

The bank's door finally opened, admitting both the bank teller and Morgan Earp. "Everybody all right?" Morgan asked.

"Think so," said Slocum. "'Cept him." He pointed to the boy on the floor.

Morgan whirled around and seemed surprised to see him. "Hey, Slocum!" he said, then shook his head. "I shoulda known," he added, grinning.

"Shoulda known what? That it was me or him?" Slocum, a half smirk on his face, pointed toward the boy on the floor. He was waking up.

Morgan shook his head. "Both, I reckon." He nodded at the floor. "That's the kid from over at the O.K. Corral, ain't it? I swear, don't know why they hired him in the first place. Kid's just bad news waitin' for a punch line."

"Reckon he's got one now," Slocum said.

Slowly, the boy had pushed himself up into a sit, and now he glared up at Slocum. Softly, he hissed, "I'm gonna get you, mister."

Suddenly, Morgan grabbed the kid's collar and jerked him to his feet. "You ain't gonna get nothin' but jail time, junior," Morgan said. "Mayhap a trip to the wood-shed, to boot!" He had already picked up the boy's gun and stuck it through his belt. Now he brought out a pair of handcuffs and slapped them on him. As he opened the door, Morgan said, "Stop up by the office later, Slocum, let Virgil take a statement, okay?"

Slocum nodded his agreement as Morgan and his prisoner went out onto the sidewalk, and Slocum heard, through the closing door, "Dadgum it, there's silver just sittin' around all over for the takin'. How come you gotta go bother the folks at the bank? And consider yourself lucky that Slocum just buffaloed you. Coulda rammed that gun a' his straight up your behind and it wouldn't have made me no never mind . . ."

Morgan's voice faded with distance, and was drowned out by the hubbub that suddenly filled the bank. Everybody began talking all at once—save for Slocum, of course—and the fat woman had revived and was now convulsed with tears and demanding that someone force brandy down her throat.

It seemed like a good time to make a getaway, which Slocum did. He went all the way up the street and back into the Oriental, where Wyatt was quietly dealing faro. Slocum got himself a table and ordered a beer.

He figured he deserved it.

He was on his second beer and just thinking that maybe he ought to go take a nap, when Will came down the stairs. He raised a hand, grinned, and headed straight for Slocum's table.

After he was seated and had ordered a beer, he said, "So, Slocum! Whatcha been up to? Get out to take some air, or you just down for a drink?"

"Oh, I've been an active hand, Will. Been over to the stable and checked the horses. Duster's fine, by the way. Strolled down the street, went over to Miss Nellie Cashman's boardinghouse and saw Mandy."

Will smirked, but Slocum cut him off. "No, just saw her. Then we went up to the bank and took care of some business before I had to stop a bank robbery, and then—"

Will raised both hands as well as his eyebrows. "What? You stopped a bank robbery? Single-handed?"

Slocum smiled. "Long story. It was that punk kid from over at the livery. Thought he looked kinda sneaky.

Just thumped him on the back of the head before he had a chance to shoot anybody, that's all." He took a long draw on his beer. At least Will hadn't asked him why he and Mandy went to the bank together. He didn't want anybody spreading rumors about his being *too* nice a fellow. Bad for the reputation.

Will shook his head. "Well, by God, Slocum! Thought you were supposed to be takin' it easy, but the first chance you get, off you go, thwartin' bank robbers!" Will rubbed his forehead. "I believe you're givin' me a headache."

Slocum laughed, and Will looked even more perplexed.

"Oh, by the way, I think Mandy's wantin' to talk to you," Slocum said.

Will brightened. "Me?"

"Don't get your hopes up, hoss. She's outta business. Retirin'."

"Does she gotta do it right now?"

"'Fraid so," Slocum said with a small grin. "'Sides, she's my girl. For the moment." Slocum wasn't yet quite ready to share. "She's wantin' to talk to you about Prescott. How you like it livin' up there and such. Think she's givin' it consideration for a place to put down fresh roots."

"Be happy to talk with her!" Will said. "Course, I'd be happy to talk with her about anything. She's sure a looker, Slocum."

Slocum nodded.

"I think she'd like Prescott, if she don't mind a little winter. We get snow up there, y'know. She thinking about buyin' or rentin'?"

"Buyin', I think." With almost ten grand in the bank, she'd be crazy not to buy, Slocum thought, but he kept his council.

"There's nice houses up there. And lots of 'em. She could get a real nice new Victorian for about a thousand. With inside water!"

"Sounds like you're the man to talk to, then. Glad I steered her to you."

"Appreciate it, Slocum. I'm always ready to talk Prescott up. But . . . She don't wanna open a house there? I mean, you know . . ."

"No, Will." Slocum shook his head. "She wants a fresh start in a new place, that's all. And you'd best keep anything you know otherwise under your hat, got it?"

Will sighed and gave his hat a tug, as if to seal it shut on all of Slocum's secrets, as well as Mandy's and his own. "Yeah, I got it. Loud and clear."

22

When Slocum woke this time, it was dark out. He lit the lamp by his bed, shook out the match, and checked his watch. Eight-thirty. He supposed it wasn't too late to take a walk up to the marshal's office and give a statement.

Slowly, favoring his shoulder and chest, he swung his legs to the floor and got out of bed.

This is ridiculous, he thought. *If I'da had half a brain, I woulda just let that son-of-a-bitchin' shirttail kid rob the damn bank and saved myself some time and trouble.*

But then he realized that if he had done that, the kid and his money—and Mandy's money, and Will's money—would be gone, too. And he would've most likely been drafted to go hunt the kid down before he did any more damage to anybody else.

Okay, going to the sheriff's office at night wasn't so bad, was it? At least, not compared to the alternatives.

He quickly checked his guns, put on his hat, and left

the room. He was halfway down the stairs when a voice from behind him called out, "Hey, buddy, wait up!"

It was Will, probably hoping for company for a beer or three.

"Hey, Will," Slocum said. "I'll join you for a beer after a while. Runnin' up the the marshal's right now to give a statement."

But Will followed him down the stairs anyway. "Statement?" he said. "'Bout bringin' in Dugan?"

"No, somethin' else." Slocum stepped off the stairs and into the bar.

"What?" Will was still right behind him.

"About this afternoon." Slocum kept walking, and waved at Wyatt as he passed the faro table. Wyatt nodded back.

"Nice job, Slocum," he said as Slocum passed.

Slocum adjusted his direction to take him out to the street, and found Will standing directly in his path.

"Nice job on what?"

Slocum sighed. "On the bank deal," he said.

"Oh. That," said Will.

Slocum didn't like Will's blasé attitude even more than he didn't like his enthusiasm. But he brushed past him and said, "Gotta go up to see Virgil for a minute, that's all. No need for you to trouble yourself. I'll be back for that beer in two shakes."

Will grunted, and Slocum left him behind. His shoulder was bothering him less and less, he noticed, the more he moved. Maybe he'd live through this deal, after all!

He crossed the street and opened the door to Virgil's office.

It wasn't so bad, after all.

He just talked, and Virgil wrote it down, and when

they were finished, Slocum read it over, then signed his name at the bottom of the page. No trouble at all. And he learned that the boy was a young cousin of the notorious Clanton outfit, and he'd just ridden into town about a week ago.

But when Slocum got up to leave, Virgil said, "Hang on a minute, Slocum. Me and my brothers been talkin'. And, well, I just talked to the territorial marshal's office."

Slocum cocked a brow. "How could you just talk to 'em? Takes two, three days to send a letter up there!"

Virgil poked his thumb at a contraption on the wall behind him. "They call it a Bell Telephone. They just put it in this mornin'. Don't rightly understand it myself, but it lets you talk to folks anywhere, long as they've got one, too."

Slocum nodded. He said, "I believe I seen one a' these things before, up to Denver not too long ago. Tombstone's gettin' real civilized these days, ain't she?"

Virgil shook his head, as if he were sad to see it come. "That she is, Slocum, that she is. But I'm gettin' off track. We discussed it, the whole of us, and we think you'd make a good deputy. One who can think for himself and act accordingly. Sorry to say it don't pay much, but we'd appreciate it if you signed on."

Slocum was taken aback, quite literally, to the point where he thumped his spine against the wall. He shook his head. "Appreciate the offer, Virgil, but I don't think so."

"Why not?"

Slocum shrugged. "Got too many places to go, too many people to see. You know."

Virgil sighed. "And you got too many lady friends dotted all over the countryside." He shook his head, then opened the top drawer of his desk and pulled out an envelope. "I s'pose I understand. Don't you wanna think it over?"

"'Fraid not, but still, thanks. Hell, it's an honor just to be asked."

Virgil handed him the envelope, which was sealed.

"What's this?"

"Reward. No, rewards, plural. For foilin' the bank job, and also for going out with Wyatt after Dugan. Your doctor bill's on the county, by the way."

Slocum started to hand the envelope back, saying, "Now, Virgil . . ."

But Virgil folded his arms and backed away. "Go buy yourself a bottle a' champagne and a gal for the night," he said with a grin. "And if you change your mind about the other . . ."

Slocum nodded his thanks and went out the door. One thing about Virgil: he was more than fair. Not much of a sense of humor, but fair right down to his bones.

Slocum walked back down to the Oriental and had gone inside before he remembered the envelope. And even then, he first sat at a table and ordered a bottle of champagne—taking Virgil's advice, or at least part of it—before he pulled the envelope from his pocket. He was about to open it when Will suddenly sat down at his table.

"Greetin's!" he said. He leaned back in his chair and thumbed his hat back, too. "All finished up with the legalities?"

"All done." Slocum slit the envelope with his nail and peered inside. Shit. Virgil wasn't fair. Virgil was generous, right down to his goddamn toenails! There were two crisp, new one-hundred-dollar bills inside.

He quickly tucked the envelope back in his pocket

and instead brought out a new pack of ready-mades. If he was going to have to share with Will, he'd rather it be a smoke and some wine, not more cash money.

The champagne arrived in an iced silver bucket, and Will didn't need an invitation to grab the first glass. Slocum smiled to himself. He guessed he didn't need a whole bottle all to himself, after all.

"Well, you were right. That was sure quick," Will said as he poured himself a second glass.

"You know," said Slocum, "if you don't watch out, you're gonna develop a taste for the finer things." He flicked a sulfur-tip and lit a smoke, then offered the pack to Will.

Will waved a hand. "Just 'cause I don't roll my own quirleys, don't mean I'm smokin' only the store-bought kind." He emptied his glass again. "Just never got the habit, I reckon." He poured out a third glass for himself.

Well, hell. Slocum supposed that he'd created a monster, and that Will was just a sponge for champagne.

"Glad to find the two of you so handy!" Mandy said from behind Slocum's back. Grinning, he turned and took her in from head to toe—and she was a sight to see, all right! She wore a brand-new, store-bought dress—pale blue and very simple. Nothing to even suggest her former line of work.

He said, "Mandy, you're a vision in that dress!"

She curtsied. "Why, thank you, Slocum! You mind if I sit down?"

He pulled out the chair next to him. Meanwhile, Will was just staring with his mouth open. Probably in shock, Slocum thought. But at least it gave Slocum the time to signal the bartender for another glass.

Mandy turned to Will. "Mister . . . I don't believe I caught your last name the last time we met."

Will stuttered, "H-Hutchins. Will Hutchins, ma'am." Even he regarded her as a lady and not some nameless whore, up from the cribs. Mandy would do just fine, Slocum thought. Just fine.

She then launched into a long list of questions about Prescott, which Will answered—at first, with a hitch in his throat, but later he relaxed and waxed poetic about his hometown. And at great length.

Slocum was tired again. And he'd be damned if he'd buy another flagon of champagne so that Mandy could nurse one measly glass while Will drank the rest like it was soda pop.

He got to his feet. "Sorry, folks, but this ol' boy needs some shut-eye," he said, and putting his hands on Mandy's shoulders, he gave her a little squeeze. He bent to her ear. "You look damn classy, Mandy," he whispered. "Like the goddamn Queen of England."

She blushed, the color rising up her neck, and giggled a little. "Why, thank you, Mr. Slocum," she said. She caught his hand before he could pull away. "I'll be up later to tuck you in."

He smiled and lifted her hand to his lips. "My pleasure, Miss Mandy," he said before he kissed it.

"Now, ain't we gettin' hoity-toity!" laughed Will, breaking the concentration of both of them, and their locked eyes.

"Aw, buy your own champagne," Slocum growled before he winked at Mandy, then turned toward the stairs.

He hadn't been in his room five minutes when Mandy rapped lightly on the door.

"It ain't locked," he called out.

The door opened, and in she walked. She looked like a rancher's daughter, or a girl from New York City, or, well, just a beautiful girl. She closed the door behind her, then turned the latch. "It is now," she said.

Slocum didn't say a word. He just held out his arms and she rushed into them.

Later, she joined him in a ready-made, and they both lay back on the sheets, naked and glistening with sweat. "There's nobody like you, Slocum. Nobody in the whole wide world."

He planted a kiss on the milky skin of her breast before he said, "Oh, there must be. Maybe over in Paris, France. Or Russia."

She giggled like a little girl. "I never been to those places, but I can just about guarantee they ain't got nothin' like you."

He smiled. "Have to take your word for it, then, Miss Mandy." He took the last drag off his smoke and ground out the butt in the ashtray. "At this point, I'd take your word for just about anythin'."

He let his hand lightly touch down on the tender flesh where her ribs met, then slowly laze down her soft, pale belly. She parted her legs slightly so that he could cup her in his palm.

She asked, "Again?"

He slipped a finger just inside her and began to rub, very gently. He was hard again, too, and he figured he might as well share the joy. He looked deep into her eyes. "If the lady wouldn't mind?"

She smiled back at him. "Oh, the lady wouldn't mind. She wouldn't mind one little ol' bit."

23

When Slocum woke the next day, she was gone, but there was a note. She was leaving on the morning stage for Prescott, it said. She'd be forever grateful, and she loved him very much.

He read the note over several times, even though it refused to change messages, but he finally put it down without a curse passing his lips. He had very much wanted to see Mandy this morning, but now he'd have to go all the way up to Prescott to do that. He hadn't planned on Prescott again until sometime next year. Maybe the next.

He sat down, sighing deeply. After feeling sorry for himself for a whole five minutes, he snapped himself out of it. "She's better off outta here anyway," he muttered as he started to dress. "And I gotta deliver those thieved horses to Monkey Springs. Mandy'll wait. I need to go over to Dallas anyhow. Then Fort Smith, over in Arkansas."

He'd "anyhow'd" himself completely out of her within

another ten minutes, when he realized that he hadn't had so much as an ache from his wound all morning long. "Now, that's a pure-dee miracle!" he said aloud, then laughed.

Even laughter didn't hurt, and he only laughed harder.

There was a knock at the door. "Come on in," he called, expecting to see Doc Goodnight, or Will, or maybe Wyatt.

He didn't, but he was close. It was Morgan. "Sorry to disturb you, Slocum," he said.

Slocum was tempted to ask him what had possessed him to do it then, but he held his tongue. He raised his brow, by way of inquiry.

"It's, well . . ." Morgan mumbled. It seemed that now he was here, he couldn't get the words out.

"What, Morgan?" Slocum demanded, in a tone meant to spook the words out of him.

It worked. "Your horses are gone," he said, all in a rush.

"What! Both of 'em?"

Morgan nodded slowly.

Slocum grabbed his hat and bolted for the stairs. It was ten-thirty now. Just how long had those horses been missing? He ought to tie a bell to Apache's saddle, he thought. No, he oughta tie Apache to his foot at night, that's what he ought to do. Why on earth, with all the horses at the O.K. to pick from, would anybody grab his two? Both of them!

He stepped off the bottom riser, half-running. He bumped straight into Wyatt and bounced back into the side of the bar.

But Wyatt only laughed. "Hey, Slocum! You okay, buddy?"

"Yeah, fine. Sorry 'bout that."

"No problem. And now . . ."

"Surprise!" the bar crowd shouted in unison.

Slocum blinked rapidly. What the hell was everybody yelling about when they should be out finding his horses?

Morgan Earp stepped up behind him. "Half the town wanted to thank you for savin' the bank yesterday, Slocum. And you can stop frettin' about your horses. They're fine."

Slocum didn't know whether to slug him or kiss him, but he didn't have time to mull it over. Wyatt turned him around again and guided him to a table where Will was already seated—and already working on a bottle of champagne. So far, he'd drunk about half of it.

Slocum sat down to a round of cheers. "Good wine?" he asked Will, and then nodded to the crowd. When they settled into drinking, he asked him, "You got any extra for me?"

"Sure!" Will crowed, oblivious to the sarcasm. "Got another bottle comin'!"

Wyatt and Morgan joined them, and Slocum ordered a ham sandwich. It didn't exactly go with the champagne, but it gave him some cushion for it to sit on.

By the time that Virgil came in to join them, Will had passed out, but other than that, it was a good time. Slocum had never had anybody throw a party for him, except when he was a little kid and his mother invited a few of the kids from school over. He remembered that during a game of pin the tail on the donkey, Joey Turnstall had thrown up on everybody—including the donkey. Well, maybe they'd twirled him too hard.

But that had been the last party anybody'd thrown for Slocum, and he couldn't say that he was too fond of them. Although this one was proving to be better—at least, no one had retched yet—because most of the attendees were already happily hammered.

At about noon, Slocum left the party and wandered out to the sidewalk, where he pulled up a bench and settled back. *That was real nice of the Earps,* he thought. *Real nice for them to throw me a soiree.* He glanced down the street, and saw Apache's handsome head, munching hay and poking out through a stall window.

"I think I'll leave," he muttered to no one in particular. Of course, he had to deliver those horses back to Monkey Springs. Those folks couldn't live without their horses forever. He'd thought it over and decided to take Red to them, too, to replace the horse that Will had shot. Red was undoubtedly a far better mount than the one that had been originally stolen, but Slocum couldn't see replacing somebody's saddle horse with something from the knacker's yard.

"Thinkin' about leavin'?" said Wyatt's voice. He had come out and was standing next to Slocum's bench, smoking.

"I must be slippin'," Slocum said. "Didn't even hear you come out."

"Ain't you heard?" Wyatt said as he motioned for Slocum to scoot over, then sat down next to him. "I can be quiet as a cat when I wanna be."

Slocum smiled. "Seems to me I did hear somethin' like that."

"Well, there you go."

They sat in silence for a few minutes while Slocum lit one of his ready-mades.

He had it half-smoked before Wyatt said, "So, you goin' or not?"

"Sounds like you're tryin' to get rid'a me," Slocum said, a hint of a smile on his lips.

Wyatt, his expression mirroring Slocum's, said, "Might wanna take it that way."

"Monkey Springs wants their horses back, don't they?"

"Reckon so."

Slocum turned to face Wyatt. "You don't mean to tell me they've got themselves a telephone machine out there, too!"

Wyatt laughed. "No, not hardly. Drifter came into town this mornin', just been through there. Said folks were gettin' antsy."

"Yeah."

"Yeah, you agree with 'em, or yeah, you're takin' the horses back?"

Slocum took a last drag on his smoke. "Both. Figure to leave in the mornin'."

They were silent for a moment as they watched a man fall head-first through the Oriental's batwing doors and tumble down in the street.

Wyatt nodded his head. "Sounds like a deal. Suppose you heard that Mandy left on the mornin' stage?"

"Yeah. She left me a letter."

"You two didn't have a fallin' out, did you?"

"Nope."

Wyatt nodded again. "Glad to hear it." He stood up and made his way over to the door. "See you later," he said with a tip of his hat.

"Back atcha, Wyatt." Slocum touched the brim of his hat, too.

The next morning, Slocum rolled out of bed at about seven, then went straight to the doc's and had his bandages changed. He figured it might be a while until he got to a place where there was a decent medical man, and after what had happened with this wound the first time, he wasn't about to take a chance on it.

Doc Goodnight pronounced him in great shape, changed his bandage, and told him that he wouldn't need any more. He was just supposed to "air it out," the doc had said, once he'd let the current dressing sit for a few days.

Relieved, Slocum set out for the livery, where he saddled all of the extra horses—including Red—that he was supposed to deliver, and Apache. He bought new halters for those that didn't have them, and clipped a lead rope to each, then tied the free end to the next horse's saddle horn. Horses trailing him in a string, he crossed the street and went into the marshal's office.

"Howdy, Virgil," he said. "Just wanted to say g'bye."

Virgil looked up from his paperwork. "Mornin', Slocum! You leavin' us so soon?" He grinned. "And without even takin' the deputy job?"

Slocum smiled back. "Now, Virgil. You boys knew I wouldn't take that job before you even asked me."

"Well, the offer's open just the same. Anytime you want."

"I'll make me a note a' that. You tell Wyatt and Morgan bye for me, too, would ya?"

Virgil nodded. "Will do. You take care a' yourself now, Slocum."

He'd said good-bye to Will last night. But now, as he led the string of horses out of town, puffing on a ready-made, he wondered if Will had been sober enough to remember it this morning. Well, he'd said it in front of the bartender, so he had a witness. He grinned.

He decided to leave town going north and cross the low mountains up a little farther, before they really turned into the Santa Ritas. Mountain climbing with Apache was one thing, but with three other horses in tow? That was a whole different kettle of fish.

He followed the dry bed of a river, once he got clear of Tombstone. He didn't remember when the river'd had water, but he'd been told that it had once fed a swamp that used to be next to Tucson, miles to the north.

Rivers were off again, on again things in the Territory. Seemed like it was either feast or famine with them. The Rio Salado that ran through Phoenix was dry as a bone for the better part of the year, but during rainy season, it regularly flooded seven miles wide. Most rivers ran underground most of the time, like the one he was following. The only way you knew it was there was the narrow line of deep-rooted foliage that rose from its path.

Monkey Springs, where he was headed, had a real spring, too. Sometimes. He supposed it'd had monkeys, too, once upon a time. He reminded himself to ask somebody, once he got there. Somebody might remember the old days.

Somebody usually did.

After a couple hours, he came to the pass that scooped out the space between this range and the next. He turned west and started toward it. He'd make Monkey Springs before nightfall, he guessed. And then he wondered if they had such a thing as a hotel.

Course, he could always just bed down in the livery, such as it was. He'd had a lot worse.

He clucked to the horses, moving them across the desert in a soft jog.

24

Slocum rode into Monkey Springs in the early evening. The ride had been uneventful and the day hadn't been too warm, which was appreciated by Slocum—and probably most of the other people in the Territory.

He took the horses to the stable and asked about lodging for himself. As he had suspected, there wasn't a hotel, but he got permission to sleep in the livery. With Apache. The hostler—who Slocum wouldn't have trusted to clean out a spittoon, let alone take care of his horses—offered the lodging free, so long as Slocum slept in the same stall with his horse.

Slocum agreed. He'd slept in worse places, and Apache could be counted on not to step on him. He hoped.

He stripped all four horses of their tack while Apache stood and waited patiently, and then he pulled Apache's tack and gave him a good grooming.

While he was currying Apache, the town sheriff

stopped by—Slocum was amazed to find him still upright—and reclaimed his horse, giving her a big, sloppy kiss on the nose. Luckily for Slocum, all he got for bringing her back was a nod and a "Thankee!"

Apparently, he stopped by the bar and the dry goods store on his way up the street, because it wasn't long before the bartender and the storekeep came down to collect their respective horses and shake Slocum's hand.

Frankly, he had liked the sheriff's attitude better.

He told the barkeep about the other horse getting shot, and asked whose it had been.

"Oh, that was Lucy Gillis's gelding. Flair, I think she called him. Shame about him gettin' kilt." The bartender shook his head. "I'll tell her, iffen you like."

Slocum thought it over for a few seconds, considered the possibilities, then said, "No, I'll tell her." He nodded toward Red and added, "I brought her a replacement mount, and I'd like to know who he's goin' to."

The bartender shrugged. "Fine by me. She lives across the street, over the dry goods. A real nice little old lady."

"Thanks," said Slocum, with a rapidly deflating sense of hope.

"You betcha," the barkeep said, much too jovially.

Shoulda broke your neck the last time I was through here, Slocum thought, and turned back to working on his horse. Behind him, he heard the bartender leave.

He finished up, patted Apache on the neck, then went to Red and stroked him. "Sounds like you're goin' to a nice little old lady, buddy," he murmured. "Sounds like you won't be doin' much work from now on. Big change, huh?"

The horse bobbed his head, and Slocum laughed. "Nice timing, boy."

* * *

Before he did anything else, he had dinner. There was a tiny café across the street, and he ducked into it. He ordered steak and potatoes with all the trimmings, and apple pie with cheese for desert. It was all delivered, in a reasonable amount of time, by an old man in a stained white apron. He was the only other soul in the place.

"You do the cookin', too?" Slocum asked as the man laid his dinner in front of him.

"Yup," the old geezer said. "Own the place, too, so if you got any complaints, I'm the man to see."

Slocum stuck out his hand. "Howdy. Name's Slocum."

The geezer took it. "I'm Arthur Gillis."

Gillis? Hadn't the bartender said that Lucy Gillis had owned the horse that was shot, and so was now Red's new owner? If so, this was likely her husband.

Well, business later. Food first!

He dug into his dinner like he hadn't seen nourishment for a week.

After all was eaten—literally—he belched loudly and got himself another cup of coffee. It was pretty good, and he figured to savor it with a smoke. As he lit his ready-made, he noticed movement in the kitchen and stepped toward it.

"Mr. Gillis?" he called.

"That's me," Gillis said as he looked up from the floor he was sweeping. "Need somethin' else?"

"No, no." Slocum shook his head. "Supper was real tasty. You fixed the steak just right. Just wanted to talk to Lucy for a minute, that's all."

Gillis frowned. "Lucy? What business you got with my Lucy?"

"Her horse was one a' the ones stolen by the Dugan gang?"

"So they say."

"Well, it got shot. I'm real sorry, and I brought her a replacement. He's over at the livery now. Bright sorrel gelding, trained up real nice."

"You shot her horse?" The old man was still stuck on that.

"No, sir, I didn't, but he got shot while we were roundin' up the Dugan gang. My partner put him out of his misery."

Slowly, the old man shook his head. "Poor, poor Lucy. She's gonna be right hurt."

"I brought her a new horse," Slocum said again, although he knew what it was like to love a horse, only to have some idiot rip it away. "Would you like me to tell her?"

"No. I'll tell her tonight. Reckon you can show her the new horse, come mornin'. Poor Lucy. She was just crazy about that Flair horse a' hers."

Leaving Gillis to sweep away his woes, Slocum went back to his table to finish his coffee and smoke. Somehow, they didn't taste as good as they had just a few minutes ago. He felt awful sorry for Lucy Gillis. He imagined her, sitting upstairs, knitting by lamplight, oblivious to the fact that her husband was about to give her the awful news about poor Flair.

He put his smoke out in the remaining coffee. He needed a beer. No, a whiskey.

He was just starting his third beer—and had just finished his second whiskey—when the idea struck him. If Lucy Gillis didn't want Red, he'd just take him and pay her for her horse. Maybe she didn't ride him at all. Maybe he was just a pet, an irreplaceable pet. But he could take Red up to Prescott and give him to Mandy. Mandy liked a good horse. Course, Prescott was pretty far away, and he'd rather be moving on to his next job, but . . .

"Mr. Slocum?" asked a melodious female voice at his left.

He turned toward it, and couldn't help taking a step back in abject shock. She was beautiful! And she was in a saloon in Monkey Springs? The only women he knew of that lived in Monkey Springs were the storekeeper's fat wife and old Lucy Gillis.

"Can I help you, miss?" he asked, touching the brim of his hat.

"If your name's Slocum, you can." She had blue eyes, fair skin, and long, dark, silky hair that hung almost to her tiny waist.

He was enchanted. He said, "At your service, miss. What can I do for you?"

She took a deep breath. "I understand you have my horse?"

"Beg pardon?"

"Do you have my horse?" she repeated slowly, as if he were feeble. "I'm Lucy Gillis."

He turned toward the barkeeper, who was laughing behind his hand. "I'm gonna kill you."

"Oh sure, a man in the hip pocket a' the Earp boys is gonna kill me." This time, the bartender laughed out loud.

"Shut up, Gary," Miss Lucy Gillis said sharply, and damned if he didn't do it!

"Pleased to make your acquaintance, Miss Lucy," Slocum said. Monkey Springs had suddenly taken on a whole new aspect for him. "Would you like to be seein' your new horse now?"

She shook her head, and her hair wafted slowly, like the current in a sluggish river. "Go ahead, Mr. Slocum. Finish your beer."

She pulled up the stool next to him and ordered a sarsaparilla. She sipped it while he sipped his beer—and tossed back his whiskey in one gulp, when she wasn't looking. He said, "I'm real sorry about your horse, Miss Lucy. But I brought you a real nice one to replace him. If he can be replaced at all, I mean."

"I'll need to see him first. And is he trained? Broke good? I don't want someone tryin' to foist a half-broke bronc on me that's gonna break my neck the first time I try to ride him."

Slocum grinned. "Oh, he's broke way better than that. I can vouch for him."

She hopped down off her bar stool. The soda pop glass in front of her was empty, and so, Slocum realized, was his beer mug. She said, "Let's go see him."

While Slocum was showing Lucy Gillis her new horse, Will was back in Tombstone, finally getting laid. She wasn't as pretty as Mandy, but she was close, he thought. Real close.

Her name was Gillian and he had picked her up down by the cribs with an offer of three dollars and a night in a hotel bed. She'd been more than willing and had given him two rides instead of just one. He thought maybe he'd tip her in the morning. Make it an even five. No, five wasn't even, was it? It'd have to be four or six. But he liked the sound of five better.

Oh, what the hell. He shouldn't have bought champagne to impress her. She would have been just as impressed with a mug of beer or a gin fizz. But right now, as she lay sleeping beside him, naked as the day she was born, he would have bought another bottle of champagne just to wake her up and start the evening over.

Gosh, she was pretty!

* * *

"Well, what d'you think of him?" Slocum asked.

Lucy said, "Hold the lamp higher, please?"

He did, and she cooed to the horse. "Hey, Red. How you doin', fella? C'mere, boy. Come to your new mama." She filled her hand with corn, held it out, and the gelding took the last few steps to lip it from her palm.

Slocum was still staring at her. She had a small, heart-shaped face, with tiny yet swollen lips—the kind they called "bee-stung." She asked him, "Do you know what his breeding is?"

It took him a second to formulate an answer. "No, Miss Lucy. Horse traders don't usually have time to fool with stuff like that if they've got the sense to know it in the first place. You ask 'em for an Arab, and every horse in their string just came over on the last boat, y'know?"

She laughed a little. "Yes, I'm afraid I do. And please, do call me Lucy. Just Lucy."

He touched his hat, tipping it slightly. "Fine. Lucy then. And I'm just Slocum."

"No first name?"

"John, but it's easier not to use it."

"All right then, Slocum." She pointed toward the horse. "I'm guessing part Morgan. What do you think?"

He smiled. "Woulda guessed that way myself, had I been asked. I'm thinkin' maybe a touch of English Thoroughbred or Arab, and a whole lot of grade stock. He's too light and thin-skinned to have any cart horse in him, and he's too fine around the edges, too. Got those little Arab tipped-in ears, too. Carries his tail high like an Arab, as well."

Lucy leaned against the side of the stall, which was to be his bedroom tonight. "Sounds like he's a pretty nice horse."

•

"I bought him to ride myself, after somebody made off with my Appy," he said. "I don't ride junk."

"I can see that," she said, a smile working its way to the corners of her lips. "What Gary said about you and the Earps. That true?"

He shrugged. "I s'pose. Known most of 'em since back in Kansas."

"You from there?"

"No. From all over, I guess. Met Doc first, up Laramie way. Course, he ain't an Earp, but he's the next best thing."

This brought out the full-fledged grin that had been working its way across Lucy's lips for the past few minutes. "I've met Doc, too. He's quite the Southern character, isn't he?"

Slocum grinned back at her. "Yeah. That he surely is. He was outta town when I was through Tombstone this time, though."

"Shame," she said, still smiling.

A thought occurred to him. "You know, you kinda remind me a' somebody. Can't say who or when, but . . . Boy howdy, it's messin' with my mind." Then something went *click*, and he said, "Did you ever dance? No offense or anything, but on the stage?"

She threw her shoulders back and lifted one skirted leg straight out before she brought her knee to her nose. She wiggled her foot, saying, "Miss Tansy's Terpsichore Temptresses."

"*That's* it!" Slocum half-shouted. "I seen you gals a year ago March, up in Denver. Say, you were swell!" He didn't mention it, but he'd had a private "dance" from two of the girls after the show. Neither of which had been Lucy, unfortunately.

She put her leg back down, and for a long moment,

they just stared at each other. He knew what he was hoping for, but he couldn't tell about her.

And then she approached him, coming across the stall. She stopped before him and opened her arms wide, putting a hand on either side of him on the rail. "I like him, Slocum," she whispered. "I believe I'll keep him."

"Good," he whispered back, and lowered his mouth to within inches of hers. "Glad to hear it. Care to stay over awhile?"

"Now that you mention it, I don't mind if I do," she whispered. "Don't mind it at all."

They kissed long and hard before they slid down into a soft bed of straw.

And Red didn't step on them once, the whole night.

Watch for

**SLOCUM AND THE WOMAN
SOLD TO THE COMANCHE**

373rd novel in the exciting SLOCUM series
from Jove

Coming in March!

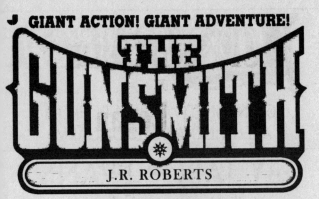

GIANT ACTION! GIANT ADVENTURE!

THE GUNSMITH

J.R. ROBERTS

penguin.com/actionwesterns

M455AS0509

LONGARM

GIANT-SIZED ADVENTURE FROM AVENGING ANGEL LONGARM.

BY TABOR EVANS

2006 Giant Edition:

LONGARM AND THE OUTLAW EMPRESS

2007 Giant Edition:

LONGARM AND THE GOLDEN EAGLE SHOOT-OUT

2008 Giant Edition:

LONGARM AND THE VALLEY OF SKULLS

2009 Giant Edition:

LONGARM AND THE LONE STAR TRACKDOWN